"That niece of yours is something."

Rae was still chuckling as she pulled at the candy in his hair.

"Ouch!"

"I'm sorry. Let me get a damp paper towel and see if I can get some of the sticky off without pulling out too much of your hair."

Luke's heart thudded against his ribs as Rae gently rubbed his hair with the wet towel. The better he got to know this woman, the more he liked her. . .and the more he wanted to know about her.

"There, I think I got it all."

"Thank you." His pulse began to race as he gazed into her blue eyes and saw them sparkle with merriment.

A giggle escaped, bringing his gaze to her lips. "Meggie does a good job with those sticky hands of hers."

Luke couldn't tear his gaze away. He wanted to kiss her. "Yes, she does. I may have to find some kind of candy that's not sticky."

"I don't think that's possible," Rae said, sounding a little breathless.

Luke inclined his head closer. "With Meggie. . .probably. . .not."

The kitchen door suddenly swung open, and Rae quickly spun toward the sink.

Luke turned around to see who'd entered the kitchen and glared at his brother.

Jake looked from Luke to Rae, who had her back to him. He shrugged. "I was trying to find Sara."

"She's *not* here," Luke informed him.

"So I see." Jake backed out of the kitchen, mouthing a silent "sorry."

JANET LEE BARTON has lived all over the southern U.S., but she and her husband plan to stay put in southern Mississippi where they have made their home for the past nine years. With three daughters and six grandchildren between them, they feel blessed to have at least one daughter and her family living in the same town. Janet loves being able to share her faith through her writing. Happily married to her very own hero, she is ever thankful that the Lord brought Dan into her life, and she wants to write stories that show that the love between a man and a woman is at its best when the relationship is built with God at the center. She's very happy that the kind of romances the Lord has called her to write can be read by and shared with women of all ages, from teenagers to grandmothers alike.

Books by Janet Lee Barton

HEARTSONG PRESENTS
HP434—Family Circle
HP532—A Promise Made

Family
Ties

Janet Lee Barton

Heartsong Presents

To my Lord and Savior for showing me the way, to the wonderful family He's blessed me with, and to the real Sunday night supper crew. I love you all!

A note from the Author:
I love to hear from my readers! You may correspond with me by writing:

Janet Lee Barton
Author Relations
PO Box 719
Uhrichsville, OH 44683

ISBN 1-58660-923-8

FAMILY TIES

Our mission is to publish an distribute inspirational products offering exceptional value and biblical encouragement to the masses.

Scripture taken from the HOLY BIBLE, NEW INTERNATIONAL VERSION®. NIV®. Copyright © 1973, 1978, 1984 by International Bible Society. Used by permission of Zondervan Publishing House. All rights reserved.

All of the characters and events in this book are fictitious. Any resemblance to actual persons, living or dead, or to actual events is purely coincidental.

PRINTED IN THE U.S.A.

one

Luke Breland didn't quite know what the problem was, but lately he just didn't like himself much. He did know that he couldn't face one more night of his own cooking and, most especially, not a night made up of only his own company. Grabbing his Stetson from the hook beside the door, he shoved it on his head and walked out onto his back porch, letting the screen door slam behind him.

He reached his pickup with long strides, started the truck, and headed for Sweet Springs, debating where to go. He had relatives all over the place and knew he would be welcomed by any one of them. But his brother, Jake, had only been married to Sara for a few months. . .and they were still considered newlyweds. More than likely Gram was being courted, as they called it, by her beau, Will Oliver, and Aunt Nora and her suitor, Michael Wellington, were probably out to dinner or at a movie.

Luke sighed deeply and shook his head. It seemed his whole family was romantically involved with someone, all except for him and his cousin, John—and he was in Santa Fe lining up support for his upcoming senatorial campaign. Like it or not, Luke was on his own.

He headed for Deana's Diner where he could get a good meal and hopefully not have to answer a lot of questions about his rotten mood.

≈

Rae Wellington became more and more frustrated as she drove down the tree-lined streets of Sweet Springs. She couldn't find her dad anywhere. He wasn't at his house; his office had been closed for several hours, and she'd checked with the hospital to see if he was on call, only to find out he wasn't. She'd even called his cell phone number to no avail. She supposed she should have let him know she was coming, but these days most of what she did was not planned.

Planning did no good. She learned that the hard way, after having her fiancé break up with her on the eve of her wedding—for her best friend, no less. She'd been left to cancel everything, return all of the wedding presents, and answer the phone calls of friends who pitied her. All in all, she thought she'd been doing pretty well through the summer. Then school started, and she found that Laura had been transferred to Zia High School, and watching Paul and her former best friend—so obviously in love—at meetings and in the halls of the high school where they all taught just intensified the pain of betrayal. She'd managed to make it through September and October, but it had become more difficult with each passing day, and finally she could take no more. This afternoon she'd put in for an immediate leave of absence, packed her car, and driven the four hours to Sweet Springs. She felt she just had to get away, at least until she could decide whether she could continue teaching at Zia High or should ask for a transfer to another school when an opening came up. Until then, all she wanted was to run into the comforting arms of her dad. And the only place she could do that was in the small town he now called home.

He'd been trying to get her to move down to Sweet Springs ever since the breakup, but Rae liked living in Albuquerque. She loved the view of the mountains from her living room window and liked the fact that it was the largest city in New Mexico, even though it would be considered small by national standards. She had no interest in moving to a tiny town like Sweet Springs—no matter how quaint it might be—and she couldn't understand why her dad wanted to live here. She was hoping to convince him to move back.

In Albuquerque there were so many choices of places to eat, deciding on where to go was sometimes a problem; here she was having a hard time even finding a café. And she needed to eat soon; otherwise the headache that had been building for the last fifty miles was going to settle in for a long stay. She should have stopped at one of the fast-food restaurants she'd passed on the way into town, but she kept remembering her dad talking a place called Deana's Diner, where he took a lot of his meals. He'd mentioned it being right downtown and having great food.

Rae turned down what she hoped was the main street in town and breathed a sigh of relief that she found the diner right across from the courthouse in the square. She eased her small car into a parking space next to a cranberry red pickup and took a minute to run a brush through her hair.

There were only a few people in the diner when she entered. An older couple sat in one booth, two teenaged couples in another, and a cowboy type sat by himself at the counter. Rae slid into a booth and began to search her handbag for some aspirin. Before she could get the purse-sized bottle open, the waitress was there with water and a menu.

"One of those days?" the waitress asked with a smile. Tall and slim, with blond hair and brown eyes, she seemed a little rushed. Her name tag read Deana, and Rae realized she must be the owner.

When Rae nodded, Deana continued. "I know the feeling. My regular waitress is on vacation; my extra help didn't show up this afternoon, and I'm left shorthanded this evening. Good thing it's been fairly slow tonight."

"Oh, I'm sorry." Rae couldn't help but sympathize with the friendly young woman.

"It happens when you own the place." Deana shrugged and smiled, pointing out the day's special on the menu. "You might think about trying the chicken and dumplings. It's my mom's recipe, and it's pure comfort food, especially when you aren't feeling up to par. I'll leave you to glance over the menu for yourself and be back to take your order in a few minutes."

"Thanks." Rae downed the aspirin quickly before studying the menu, but her mind was already made up. Those chicken and dumplings did sound awfully good.

æ

Oblivious to his surroundings, Luke waited for his order to come. He stared into his iced tea and sighed deeply. He seemed to be sighing a lot lately. He wasn't sure when this mood he was in had started, but as he thought back over the past few months, it seemed to have begun around the time all this romancing in his family became obvious. Oh, he was happy for them all; he really was. But it'd made him realize something about himself that he'd been ignoring for years. He was plain old lonesome. He couldn't deny it any longer. He wanted a family of his own—longed for a love of his own.

Fat chance of that happening. He'd dated most of the eligible women in the county, and it just never worked out. Most of them were hoping to find someone to take them out of the area, and Luke's roots went deep. He wasn't moving anywhere.

The ranch he helped run had been in his family for several generations, and he couldn't imagine doing anything else. No, he was going to have to come to grips with the fact that he might be single the rest of his life—and a few months ago, he had never given it a thought. But now. . .now, he was a pitiful excuse of a cowboy, crying in his iced tea. Luke shook his head and sighed again before his sense of humor kicked in; then he chuckled to himself.

Deana, the diner's owner, walked up just then. Setting down the chicken-fried steak he'd ordered, she peered at him closely. "You okay, Luke?"

Luke nodded. Yes. He was all right. So what if he didn't

have a romance of his own going on? The Lord had blessed him in many ways. And if the Lord meant for him to have a mate, he'd just trust Him to bring a stranger here to Sweet Springs, 'cause Luke figured that was the only way he was going to find her—whoever she was.

He grinned up at Deana. "I'll be better after I eat this meal. But I could ask you the same. Seems you are a little understaffed tonight, Dee."

"You're just a master of understatement, aren't you?" she said before hurrying across the room, her order pad in hand.

Luke gave his attention to the meal sitting in front of him. He bowed his head and prayed silently before picking up his fork. He did love chicken-fried steak.

&

When Deana came back to take her order, Rae went with her suggestion of chicken and dumplings. She could use some comfort right now. She'd been hoping for a comforting hug from her dad, but that would have to wait until she located him—if she ever did.

Deana promised to bring her meal right out, and Rae was glad she'd ordered the day's special when it was set before her only minutes later, piping hot and smelling absolutely delicious. She ate slowly, savoring each bite, and wondered what to do next. She really didn't want to spend the evening parked in her dad's driveway waiting for him to come home. Hopefully, by the time she finished her meal, he'd be there.

She did feel a little awkward eating alone in a strange town, but she tried not to show it. She watched Deana as she moved from one table to the other, taking care of her diners. The teenagers didn't seem in any hurry to leave but hadn't ordered a lot from what she could see. The older couple got up to leave just as a young family of four came in.

The cowboy at the counter seemed lost in his thoughts as he ate his meal, and Rae, man-wary as she was, couldn't help but be surprised that her gaze kept coming back to rest on him. He was tall—she could tell that from the way his long legs wrapped around the counter stool he sat on—and he was very broad shouldered. When Deana stopped to fill his iced tea glass, he thanked her in a deep, husky voice. She watched as Deana leaned over the counter and said something that made him smile, and Rae wondered idly if they were seeing each other.

Most probably they were. It seemed everyone she knew was the other half of a couple, except for her. She didn't know what she'd done to make the Lord mad, but she was sure He must be. First her mother died while she was in high school, and she and her dad were left to take care of each other. Last year her dad decided to move here. Rae shook her head. She wasn't going to let herself go down that road again. Her dad loved her. When he'd moved away, he thought she'd be happily married in a few months. He couldn't have known that her dreams for the future would come crashing down around her.

"How was it?" Deana broke into her thoughts, filling her water glass. "How about some dessert and coffee?"

"It was wonderful. Just what I needed," Rae answered. "I don't have any room for dessert, but coffee sounds good."

"Coming right up." Deana took her plate and headed back to the counter.

Rae wondered if her dad was finally home and decided to call his house once more. She couldn't help feeling disappointed when there was no answer. She flipped the top down on her cell phone and dropped it back into her handbag just as Deana came back with her coffee.

"You just passing through or are you visiting?" Deana asked.

"Visiting, if I can ever catch up with my host. You wouldn't happen to know Dr. Michael Wellington, would you?"

"Dr. Mike? Sure. He's in here nearly every day. He's not home?"

Rae could tell Deana was curious about why she was trying to find him. Ordinarily, she'd say it wasn't any of the other woman's business, but the diner owner had been very nice, and she might have an idea of where her dad could be. "He's my dad. I guess I should have let him know I was coming. It never dawned on me that he might not be home."

Deana inclined her head. "Hmm. He's not at the hospital, either?"

Rae shook her head. "No. And of course, his office has been closed for several hours."

"Maybe I can help you locate him." Deana turned toward the counter. "Hey, Luke. We could use your help over here."

Rae got her first really good look at the man as he unwound his legs from the stool and stood up. She tried to ignore the way her heart jumped as she watched the tall, handsome cowboy arch an eyebrow at Deana and smile as he crossed the room toward them.

❧

Luke wondered how he could have missed seeing the young lady sitting in the booth by the door. He must be slipping big time not to have noticed the nicely dressed, dark-haired woman when she came in. She surely wasn't here when he arrived. Who was this stranger in town? *Stranger?* Luke idly wondered if the Lord had already answered his prayer, then dismissed the ridiculous thought. Most likely, she took a wrong turn and just wanted directions. He picked up his Stetson and held it close to his side as he ambled over to her table. It was a pretty sure guess that she hadn't come to find him.

"Sure thing, Dee. What can I do for you two ladies?" he asked, smiling down at her.

"Luke, this is. . ." Dee turned to Rae and grinned.

"Rae Wellington," the stranger finished for Dee, her voice light and lilting.

"Nice to meet you, Rae," Dee said and patted Luke's shoulder. "And this big, ugly cowboy is Luke Breland. He knows everyone for miles around."

"Hi." Rae smiled up at him.

As Luke smiled down at her, a delicate pink color seemed to spread up her neck and onto her cheeks, and he had a feeling she might be embarrassed that Dee called him over. "Pleased to meet you, Rae."

"She's Dr. Mike's daughter," Dee added. "And she can't find him. Do you have any idea where he might be?"

Was she kidding? Of course he had an idea where Michael might be, and she knew it. He glanced from Dee to Rae. He could see the resemblance to Michael now; only she was a much more feminine version of her father. Delightfully so, with shoulder-length, dark, curly hair, and big blue eyes. She was very pretty. But there was a vulnerability in her eyes that caught him by surprise and called to him—bringing out every protective urge he had—to come to her aid if need be, in any way he could.

"He could be at Aunt Nora's or Gram's. I'll call around and see if I can find him." He pulled out his cell phone, flipped it open, and punched in his aunt's phone number. When her answering machine came on, he ended the call without leaving a message and started to dial his grandmother's number. Before he completed the call, the bell over the diner's door jingled, and Michael and Aunt Nora walked in, laughing about something.

He snapped the phone shut and stuck it in his pocket, watching the changing expressions on Rae's face. Her countenance quickly changed from what appeared to him as excitement, then confusion, and finally happiness.

"Daddy!" Rae scooted out of the booth and hurried to her father.

"Rae!" The joy on Michael's face told anyone watching just how happy he was to see his daughter. He enveloped her in a hug. "You're here! I wasn't expecting you until Thanksgiving! What a wonderful surprise."

"Well, I guess we don't need your detective services after all, Luke." Dee nudged him on the shoulder before hurrying over to the register where the teens were lined up to pay.

Luke shrugged, but his gaze was on Rae, and he thought he saw tears in her eyes just before she turned her face into her father's chest. Feeling a little like an intruder, he stood to the side and glanced down at his aunt.

Aunt Nora had a smile on her face, but Luke thought she seemed a little apprehensive until Michael pulled her forward to introduce her to Rae. His aunt's smile grew wider then, and Luke told himself he must have been imagining things.

"Rae, Honey, I'd like you to meet Nora Tanner." Michael gazed into Nora's eyes and smiled. "She's made my move to Sweet Springs a wonderful decision."

"I'm so pleased to meet you, Rae," Nora said graciously. "Your father talks about you all the time. I know he's thrilled to see you."

"I certainly hope so. I didn't give him any advance notice." Rae smiled at her father and glanced back to Nora. "But, I feel at a disadvantage. . . . Daddy hasn't told me about you."

Suddenly, Luke felt uncomfortable. Both women were being very nice to each other, but something didn't seem quite right, and he wasn't sure he wanted to know what it was. He decided to take his leave and go home. But as he moved to go pay for his meal, Michael caught him by the arm.

"You leaving, Luke? Might as well stay and have some pie and coffee with us."

Before he could answer, his aunt chimed in, "Oh, yes, Luke. Please join us."

Luke's "no" was on the tip of his tongue when he glanced at his aunt and changed his mind. He knew he wasn't imagining the expression in her eyes this time. It was a call to family loyalty and support, and he couldn't ignore it.

Resigned to the fact that he wasn't going anyplace for a little while, he gave in. "Dee's apple pie is hard to resist. Guess I'll join you after all."

When his aunt and Michael took one side of the booth, Rae glanced at Luke and quickly slid to the far end of the bench. Luke slid in beside her, keeping a safe distance between them. She sure was pretty. And she smelled real good. But the warm look she'd given her dad when she first spotted him had become cool when he'd introduced her to Aunt Nora. Luke suddenly realized Rae was anything but happy about her dad and his aunt seeing each other.

He hoped he was reading things wrong. Michael was the best thing to happen to his aunt in years. And they were happy together—anyone could see that. No one seemed to know quite what to say next, and Luke was relieved when Dee came to take their order.

❧

Still full from the meal she'd just eaten, Rae only asked for a refill of her coffee. When she glanced across at her father, she couldn't help smiling at the grin on his face. He was as glad to see her as she was to see him; she had no doubt of that. Still, it hurt that he hadn't told her about this woman he obviously cared about. Nora Tanner was a lovely woman—in her mid-fifties, Rae guessed. She had softly highlighted hair and was slim and elegantly dressed. Why hadn't her father mentioned that he was dating someone, and. . .how long *had* they been seeing each other?

Rae tried to smile as they gave their orders, but she knew it was strained. She felt tense sitting there with two strangers her father seemed to know so well—not to mention how nervous she felt sitting next to the broad-shouldered, handsome cowboy.

"When did you get into town, Honey?" her dad asked.

Relieved that he'd brought her out of her thoughts, Rae glanced at her watch. "A couple of hours ago. I went by your house and your office, and I even checked with the hospital. I could just picture us passing on the interstate and not knowing it. . .you to see me and me to see you."

Everyone chuckled, and the tension eased somewhat as Deana—or Dee, as Luke called her—brought back their dessert orders and refilled Rae's coffee.

"That might well have happened," he continued. "I've been telling Nora how much I've missed you and needed to get up to Albuquerque to see you, haven't I, Nora?"

"Yes, you have." Nora smiled at Rae. "He's missed you a great deal. He's been wishing you would join him here in Sweet Springs."

"Any chance of that happening, Honey? Think you could give up the city life for this close-knit little community? You'd love it here. I know you would."

"Oh, wait, Dad. I'm just here on a visit." Rae smiled and shook her head. She was well aware that everyone who lived in Albuquerque thought *they* owned the mountain range that rose so magnificently over the city, but that didn't stop her from claiming it for her own. "You know how much I love my Sandia Mountains."

"I do," he agreed. "But there's much to love here. Just wait and see. I guess you are only here for the weekend?"

Rae took a sip of her coffee. How did she answer that? She hadn't told him about taking a leave of absence from work. When she left home, she'd been planning on staying for several weeks, maybe all the way through the holidays, or as long as it took to talk her father into moving back to Albuquerque, but now. . .

"I have to make rounds at the hospital in the morning, but after that I'll try to show you as much as I can so you'll know why I love it here," he added.

"I'm taking some personal time off." She watched her dad raise an eyebrow her way and study her closely, but he kept quiet. "I'll stay through the next week, if you don't mind having me underfoot. I'm not sure after that."

Rae just couldn't bring herself to commit to more than that right now. Much as she'd been looking forward to seeing her father, it was obvious that this visit wasn't going to end quite as she'd envisioned it—with her father agreeing to move back to Albuquerque.

"What do you do?" Luke asked, smiling at her.

Thankful that someone broke the silence that had suddenly fallen, Rae returned his smile. He did have *such* beautiful brown eyes. And when he smiled, they seemed to light up from somewhere deep inside.

"I teach school," Rae informed him, trying to pull her gaze away from his and feeling a little breathless.

"What grade?"

"Ninth."

"Whoa. Not an easy grade to handle, I would imagine."

"Oh, I don't know. I think the first year of high school is probably easier than junior high. I taught that for a year and nearly bailed out." Rae grinned over at her dad. "Remember that year?"

He nodded. "I remember it well. But you got a grip on everything after a few months and went on to teach some of those same kids their first year in high school."

Rae smiled. "You're right. I did."

"Well, I admire anyone who teaches," Nora said, shaking her head. "I know I wouldn't have the patience."

"What is it you do, Nora?" Rae couldn't curb her curiosity about the woman.

Nora smiled and shook her head. "Not much."

"That's not true," her father argued. "Nora does a lot of the behind-the-scenes kind of stuff. She heads the volunteer program at the hospital; she's very active at church and with her family."

"And you don't have a job?"

"No. I've been very fortunate in that I didn't have to work—and very foolish in that I didn't always use my free time wisely." Nora glanced at Dad, and he put his arm around her, drawing her close. "But I'm trying to change all of that, with the help of the Lord. . .and Michael."

Rae almost caught her breath at the expression of love that passed between her dad and Nora. It was as if you could reach out and actually touch it. If she'd wondered if this was just a fleeting romance for him, she no longer had to guess about it. He was in love with this woman. She wished she could be happy for him, but try as she might, happy was the last thing she felt. And the strain of hiding it was building.

"Michael, your daughter seems exhausted." Nora motioned in Rae's direction. "I think it's time you showed her the way to your house from here."

Her father fixed his attention on Rae. "You do seem pretty tired, Honey. How about you follow me home, Rae, then you can start settling in while I take Nora home."

"No, Michael. If Luke doesn't mind, I'll ask him to take me home. There's something I'd like to talk to him about, anyway. And Rae has waited long enough to have you to herself. Luke, you don't mind, do you?"

"I'll be glad to take you home, Aunt Nora. It's on my way."

two

Luke was relieved when they said their good-byes. He'd begun to feel a little uncomfortable again. Only this time he didn't know if it was because of the two women's reaction to each other or because he was fighting the undeniable attraction he felt for a woman who clearly had no desire to leave *her* mountains—or Albuquerque. He left Deana's Diner in the same frame of mind he'd been in when he got there. Longing for something he'd probably never have.

Luke walked Aunt Nora to his pickup and opened the door for her. He always forgot how small a woman his aunt was until he stood right beside her. At just a little over five feet, she didn't even reach his chin. Her short, highlighted hair was just beginning to show some signs of silver threads; still, she was a lovely woman. She always appeared well put together, whether she was dressed for church or riding out on the ranch. For a long time he'd thought her one of the most self-centered women he'd ever known, but she'd changed so much in the past few months. She seemed softer, more vulnerable somehow. He saw her cast a wistful glance back toward the diner before she turned to him and smiled.

"I'm sure Michael and Rae have a lot to catch up on," she said as he helped her into the truck. "They certainly don't need my company tonight."

"Oh, I think Michael would have liked for you to stay." Luke shut the passenger door and hurried around to his side, continuing the conversation when he got in the pickup. "His daughter—"

"Wouldn't," Nora finished for him. "It seemed to upset her that Michael hadn't told her anything about me."

"She seemed kind of uptight, but that was even before you and Michael showed up. I think she was just a little upset because she couldn't find him and didn't know what to do about it."

"Hmm." Nora sighed deeply.

Luke glanced over at his aunt as they headed out of town. She was chewing her bottom lip, which was totally unlike her. He'd rarely seen his aunt flustered. "Are you all right, Aunt Nora?"

"I'm fine, Dear. Just a little nervous, I guess." She smiled at him. "I have a secret for you to keep, Luke."

Luke groaned inwardly. He hated when people confided in him and asked him not to say anything. But it seemed to be his lot in life. Everyone seemed to want to tell him their secrets, problems, or dreams. No sense in fighting it. "What is it, Aunt Nora? You and Michael elope tonight?"

She burst out laughing. "No. But you're close. The subject of marriage has come up. We're thinking about it."

"That's wonderful!" Luke grinned at her. It was good news. Michael had been wonderful for Nora. That they were in love was no secret to anyone who saw them together for any length of time. "Why are you nervous?"

"I'm not sure how Rae will react to the news. I hope Michael doesn't mention it tonight. I'd like her to get to know me first." She paused and peered out the window. "I think."

Luke chuckled. "Aunt Nora, it will be fine. I'm sure she wants her dad to be happy. And you two make each other very happy."

Nora bobbed her head. "We do, don't we? Still, she's an only child, and I'm sure it's not easy to think about someone taking her mother's place. Plus she's had some heartache in her life recently. . . ."

"Oh?" Luke was aware he was being nosy, but he couldn't help wondering what kind of heartache Rae had suffered. There was something about her. . . .

"I think she just needs some attention from her father right now." Nora didn't elaborate any further. Obviously, she wasn't telling what she knew.

Luke shrugged. "Maybe. But don't you worry, Aunt Nora. I'm sure she'll come around once she sees how much Michael cares about you. Surely she wouldn't want to cause problems for her dad."

"Luke, would you make her feel at home in Sweet Springs? Show her around some when Michael is at work? Introduce her to some of the family who are her age?"

"But—"

"Luke, she isn't ready to get to know me yet. You saw her reaction at Deana's. I don't want to force myself on her. Please."

Luke always had a hard time resisting a "please" from a lady. And Nora seemed to need his support right now. "All right, Aunt Nora. I'll see what I can do. No promises, though."

"Thank you, Dear."

Luke sighed and turned into the drive leading to Nora's ranch house. "You're welcome."

❧

Rae was relieved to finally have her father to herself. She grinned at him from across the table. "You look wonderful, Dad. I've missed you so much!"

He reached over and drew her hands into his. "I've missed you too, Honey. I'm so glad to see you. Now, tell me about this personal time you're taking."

Rae didn't want to talk about it here and now. "Can we discuss it at home, Dad? I am a little tired."

"Of course we can." Her father got up immediately and waited for her to scoot out of her side of the booth. "Let me pay Dee, and we'll be on our way."

Rae pulled on the lightweight jacket she'd brought in with her and waited for her dad to join her again. Deana waved from the cash register, and Rae waved back. It'd been nice of the woman to try to help her. "Thanks, Deana!"

"Anytime. And just call me Dee. Nearly everyone else around here has ever since your dad started calling me that."

Dad grinned and shrugged. "You started calling me Dr. Mike, and now so do lots of other people."

Dee chuckled and nodded. "You're right. I did. I hope you have a nice stay here, Rae."

"Thank you." Rae hoped she did too. But seeing how settled in her dad seemed to be, and how happy he seemed with a new woman in his life, she wasn't so sure.

Her dad walked her to her car and hurried to his own after telling her to follow him. Rae had found his house earlier, but she was glad to have him lead the way. She was impressed with his choice of homes and was anxious to see the inside. It was in a very nice subdivision, backed up to a golf course, but she was a little surprised by the style he'd chosen. Their two-story home in Albuquerque had been quite traditional, while this was a beautiful, sprawling adobe hacienda.

Almost as soon as she stopped in his driveway, her dad was there to help bring in her luggage. One glance at her bags had him turning to her with a grin. "You *are* going to stay awhile, aren't you?"

"I'm not sure, Dad. I just don't know." Rae watched him pull the two heaviest suitcases out of the trunk and move to the side. She retrieved a couple midsized cases and followed him up the walk to the front door.

He unlocked and opened the door, then picked up the luggage he'd set down beside it. "I'll bring in the rest after I see you to your room. I hope you like it. Nora helped me furnish it."

Oh, thrill, Rae thought, then immediately chastised herself. She didn't know anything about this woman, and it was way too early to form an opinion about her. Just because she didn't like the way Nora gazed at her dad was no reason to dislike her, but it sure hadn't helped Rae want to be best friends with her.

"Dad, it's beautiful!" She took in the tiled entryway and the great room just ahead. The stucco walls seemed to be washed with just a hint of yellow, giving the room a warm and inviting atmosphere. The rich brown leather couch and chairs facing the corner fireplace beckoned one to sit. Although the room had a masculine feel to it, a woman's touch was evident; there were flowers on the coffee table and several other items around the room that made it feel homey.

"Thank you, Honey. I'm glad you like it. Let's get your things to your room. Then I'll make us some hot chocolate, and we can catch up."

"Sounds wonderful." Rae followed her father down a wide hall to the left of the entryway. She supposed the kitchen was to the right.

When her dad opened the door to her room, she caught her breath. Decorated in her favorite colors of butter yellow and aqua, it was lovely. She couldn't have done a better job of decorating it herself. More of a suite than a room, it was spacious enough to have a sitting area facing French doors that opened to a courtyard. It even had its own bathroom with a whirlpool and separate shower.

"It is beautiful, Dad."

He set her cases in the dressing area and grinned at her. "I'm glad you like it, Honey. I want you to feel this is your home too."

Rae blinked away the tears that suddenly threatened and hugged her dad. "Thank you."

He cleared his throat and embraced her. "I'll just go get the rest of your things. Make yourself at home and find out where everything is. I'll meet you in the kitchen. Just head back to the entryway, then straight through."

Rae did as instructed and made her way down the hall, peeking briefly into the other bedrooms. There were two more—also tastefully decorated—each facing the center courtyard. At the end of the hall, a side door led outside. A matching door across the way opened to the other wing. Rae decided to take her dad's advice and explore. Instead of making her way back down the hall, she went outside to the courtyard—which was absolutely gorgeous. It had a view of the golf course behind the house and a pool set in the center. Although it was too cool to use it now, she could just imagine taking a dip in midsummer. There was a wrought-iron table with chairs up front, close to what she assumed was the kitchen.

She crossed the flagstone walk and entered the other wing of the house. At the end was one huge suite she imagined was her father's. The room beside it was a study, warm and welcoming with its walls of filled bookshelves. The next room was indeed the kitchen, with both the great room and dining room opening off it. It was spacious, as all the rooms in this house seemed to be.

Her dad must have sensed her presence as she stood in the doorway, because he turned and motioned her into the room.

"Mmm, that smells just like Mom used to make." She took a stool at the kitchen island where her dad was stirring his mixture on the cooktop.

"Let's just hope it tastes as good." He poured the hot, aromatic mixture into mugs and handed Rae hers.

She blew on the steaming liquid before taking a sip, all the while wondering how to broach the subject that had been on her mind since she'd first seen her dad enter the diner with Nora. "It tastes just like Mom's."

Dad chuckled. "Good. 'Cause I taught Mom how to make hers."

"You taught Mom how to make hot chocolate? She was a great cook, Dad."

"Yes, she was," he agreed. "But when we first married, she made hot chocolate from those instant packet things."

"Oh."

There was a long silence as they sipped from their cups. "Dad, why didn't you tell me about Nora?"

"I didn't know how. You've been hurting over your breakup, and I wasn't sure how you would react to the fact that I'm seeing someone."

"It's hard to think about anyone taking Mom's place."

"No one could take your mother's place in my heart, Rae—"

"Oh, good." Rae sighed with relief. "I was afraid it was serious between you and Nora."

He set down his mug and reached out to cup his daughter's chin in his hand. "Honey, you didn't let me finish. It *is* serious between us. Nora is making her own place in my heart. Your mother was my first love, and she will always own a big chunk of my heart. But she didn't want me to be alone the rest of my life, Rae. She told me to find someone else. . .I just never thought I would."

"It's that serious?"

"Yes, Rae, it is. I care deeply about Nora."

Rae stared into her cup, willing away the tears that threatened. *Dear Lord, am I to lose Daddy, too?*

"Honey, you'll like Nora if you give her a chance. Please say you'll try."

Rae took a sip from her cup. She would try, but she didn't hold out much hope that she would ever like Nora. "I guess this means I don't have any chance of talking you into moving back to Albuquerque."

Her father smiled and shook his head. "Even if I hadn't found Nora, Honey, I love Sweet Springs. You will too. Just mark my words. Now tell me, how long of a break do you have?"

"I took a leave of absence until after the first of the year.

And I'm not sure I can go back even then. I may have to try to get on at another school."

"What happened? I thought you were happy there."

"I was. And I thought I could handle working at the same school with Paul. I just avoided him as much as possible. I was doing pretty well until I had to deal with the fact that Laura was teaching at Zia High this year and. . .I saw them together every day." She choked back a sob. "I just couldn't handle it, Daddy."

He came around the kitchen island and gathered her into his arms. "Oh, Honey. I'm sorry he hurt you so badly."

Rae sniffed. "I took the time off hoping that I'll be able to handle it by the time I go back, but I'm not sure. . . ."

"Don't worry about it right now. It might be better to get a fresh start and find a new school. You take as much time as you need to make up your mind about what to do. Maybe you'll decide to teach in a small—"

"Dad. You know I love Albuquerque. I can't see me ever settling in a small town."

"Well, I can hope you change your mind. In the meantime, I'll try to talk you into staying until after the holidays."

Rae wasn't sure what she was going to do. She didn't seem to fit anywhere anymore. But the thought of facing Thanksgiving and Christmas alone was almost more than she could bear. "I'll see."

❧

Luke sat watching the news, folding the clothes in the basket at his feet. Good thing he'd thrown them in the dryer before he'd gone into town. He was out of clean socks. How that could be always amazed him—he bought new ones nearly every time he visited that new superstore on the outskirts of town. Did the washing machine really eat them? Or did the dryer blow them out the vent?

He finished folding the last pair of socks and put everything back in the laundry basket to take upstairs later. Leaning back in his chair, he took a drink from the coffee cup he'd set on the end table and watched the next day's forecast.

According to the weatherman, tomorrow was going to be a beautiful day. It might be a nice day to spend with a lovely lady. Aunt Nora had given him a good excuse to call Rae. In fact, he'd promised her he would. But for the first time he could ever remember, he was nervous about asking a woman out. He had a feeling Rae wasn't going to like him any more than she seemed to like his town or his aunt. And the last person he needed to get involved with was a city girl. But Aunt Nora had asked him, and he sure didn't want anything hurting her and Michael's relationship. And she seemed afraid Rae might do that. Maybe Nora was right. From what he'd seen tonight, Rae didn't seem to take to Nora, but maybe she had something else on her mind. After all, he didn't know a thing about her. Still, he'd made a promise. He had to keep it.

He took a long swig from his cup before picking up the phone and dialing. It rang once, twice—

"Hello?"

"Dr. Mike?" Well, of course it was Michael. He'd dialed the man's home. Who'd he expect would answer it? Rae probably wouldn't be answering her dad's phone in a town where she knew no one.

"Yes, Luke. Did you get Nora home all right? Is something wrong?"

"No, nothing's wrong. I got Aunt Nora home just fine. I was actually calling to talk to your daughter. I thought I might show her around tomorrow morning since you have to make rounds at the hospital."

"Luke! That's a great idea. Let me get her."

Although it seemed longer, Luke was certain only a few seconds passed before Rae came to the phone.

"Hello?"

"Hi, Rae. Umm, listen, I was thinking that with your dad having to work tomorrow morning, maybe I could show you around town. . .introduce you to some people. . ." Luke hoped he didn't sound as nervous as he felt. He'd never had trouble talking to anyone before. He couldn't believe how awkward he felt as he waited for her answer.

"You don't have to work?"

"Well, we just finished with the fall roundup. Things are pretty calm on the ranch right now. I can take off a few hours."

There was quiet on the line. "Rae?"

"Yes, I'm here. And thank you for the offer. That way Dad won't feel bad about working tomorrow. And I'd like to be able to find my way around while I'm here. What time would you want to get started?"

Luke was an early riser, but Rae had appeared tired this evening. It wouldn't hurt to let her sleep in. "How about ten o'clock? I could show you around for awhile, and then we could grab some lunch somewhere."

"That's fine. Do you want me to meet you in town? I can find my way back there."

"No. I'll pick you up. You get some rest, you hear? I'll see you tomorrow."

"I. . .thank you. I'll see you in the morning."

A clunk indicated that she'd hung up, and Luke replaced the receiver of his phone. She didn't sound real excited about spending the day with him. . .but she'd agreed. And he'd kept his promise to his aunt. And that was that. But hard as he tried the next few hours, flipping channels on the television, putting up his neatly folded clothes, and ironing a shirt for the next day, he couldn't get Dr. Mike's daughter out of his mind.

≈

"That was nice of Luke," her dad said when Rae joined him at the sink.

"It was." Rae picked up a dish towel and began to dry their cups, feeling both a little excited and somewhat apprehensive at the same time. The only reason she'd accepted Luke's offer for the next day was because it was obvious her dad wanted her to. The way she'd been feeling about men lately, there couldn't be any other reason—of that she was certain. No matter how nice he seemed or how handsome he was.

"He's a good man and a hard worker."

"And he's Nora's nephew?"

"Yes. It's a big family. . .the Brelands and the Tanners. You'll love them all."

Obviously, her father did. She wasn't sure she would. They were Nora's family, after all.

"His brother, Jake, and cousin, John, have a law firm in town," Michael continued. "Right now Jake is running it while John is thinking of running for the senate next year."

"For state senator?" Rae asked.

He shook his head. "United States senator."

"That's quite a goal for a man from such a small town."

"If anyone can make it, John can. He'll have my vote, that's for sure."

It seemed that Luke's brother and cousin had loftier goals than he did. But he seemed nice, and he had been willing to help her find her dad. She wondered about the ranch he'd mentioned.

"What exactly does Luke do? He's happy just being a cowboy?"

Her dad threw back his head and laughed. "There's nothing wrong with being content to be a cowboy, Honey. But Luke isn't just a cowboy—his family owns a lot of land around here. . .and all over the state. Luke helps his uncle run the ranch holdings. Actually, Ben is semiretired, and Luke mostly runs things. And he's very good at it."

Her dad drained the sink and dried his hands. "I was going

to ask Nora to show you around, but I think she had some kind of meeting tomorrow."

"Well, now you don't need to worry about me tomorrow . . .and you don't have to bother Nora. Luke said he'd show me around and we'd grab some lunch somewhere." Rae really didn't want to go sightseeing with Luke tomorrow, but it would be better than having Nora show her around. She sent up a quick prayer. *Thank You, Lord. I know I have to accept the fact that Dad cares about her, but I am so glad I don't have to spend my first day here out sightseeing with her.*

"Good. I'll plan to grill supper tomorrow night." He wrapped his arms around her. "It's going to be so good having you here, Honey. I've missed you. And I want you to get to know Nora better. I hope you'll decide to stay until after the holidays."

"I'll think about it, Dad."

"Want to watch the news with me?"

Rae shook her head. "Not tonight. I think I'll go on to bed. It's been a long day."

Dad turned out the overhead light as they headed toward the great room. "I hope you sleep well tonight. And, Rae?"

"Yes, Dad?"

"Honey, Paul doesn't deserve you. I know you are hurting now. But he wasn't in God's plan for you. In time, you'll get over him, and you'll find the man who *is* meant for you."

Rae choked back the tears that threatened and reached up to kiss him on the cheek. "Thank you, Daddy. I needed to hear that. See you in the morning."

Rae held the tears at bay until she reached her room; then she fell across the bed and let them flow freely as she gave herself over to self-pity. Everything her dad said was true . . .but still, it hurt to have lost Paul and her best friend. Now she was losing her father too. And she missed her mother more all the time.

How much more could she take? *Lord, You said You wouldn't give us more than we can bear, but I don't think I can bear much more.* Rae sniffed. *Do You hear me, Lord? I'm tired of losing people I love.* Sometimes she wondered if He'd stopped listening to her. She couldn't blame Him. . .she hadn't been talking to Him much lately. Not nearly as much as she used to. . .or as much as she needed to.

She cupped her hand around her mouth and shook her head. And whose fault was that? Hers. With fresh tears streaming down her face, she whispered, "Please help me, Lord, to feel close to You again. . .and to accept the changes in my life. In Jesus' name, amen."

three

Luke had been up for several hours when the phone rang. His caller ID indicated it was from Michael's house. Somehow he wasn't surprised. He'd figured Rae would find a reason to back out of letting him show her around. But it wasn't Rae at the other end of the line; it was Michael.

"Luke?" Michael continued without waiting for him to answer. "There's no need for you to come pick Rae up. I'm going to take her to Deana's for breakfast before going to work. She'll just explore around town for an hour or two until you get there."

The deep disappointment he'd felt at Michael's first words took him by surprise—as did the relief he felt that Rae *wasn't* canceling on him. Luke released a deep breath and leaned back in his office chair. "There's no need for her to explore on her own. I was going to eat at the diner before I came to pick her up, so meeting you there will be fine with me. I was just getting ready to head out myself."

"Okay, we'll see you there. And, Luke, thanks for offering to show her around."

Luke chuckled. "Now, you know it's really a hardship to take a day off to show a lovely lady around town, Michael."

"Yeah. Well, still, I really appreciate it. She's had a hard time of it the past few months. Ahh—see you in town."

"See—" The sudden click on the line told Luke that Michael had hung up. Maybe Rae had come into the room, and he didn't want her to hear their conversation. Luke couldn't help wondering what kind of hard time she'd had. She did appear vulnerable to him, but he figured it was because she hadn't known Michael was seeing his aunt. Maybe that had nothing to do with it, and Aunt Nora had nothing to worry about.

He turned his computer off and took a last drink of his now-lukewarm coffee before making his way to the kitchen. He rinsed out the tall mug and switched the pot off before crossing the room to grab his Stetson and pull on a denim jacket. Pulling the back door shut, he let the screen door bang behind him and headed for his pickup.

Luke took the county road toward town. It was a cool morning, but sunny and bright. He figured it'd get into the sixties later in the day, but for now he turned on the heater to take the chill off. He loved this time of year. The crispness of the air never failed to invigorate him, but this morning he wondered if his good mood was coming from the weather or the anticipation of spending the day with Rae Wellington.

Probably the latter, he admitted to himself, although he wasn't sure why. He knew little about Rae, except that she was taking time off from teaching high school, loved her hometown, and had evidently been hurt in some way. And, of course, that his aunt was worried about Rae's reaction to Michael seeing her, but that could have been just because he hadn't told her he was seeing anyone—or any number of other possibilities.

All he was sure of was that today he was going to enjoy showing Rae around. No matter that he was also attracted to her and that he'd like to get to know her better. There wasn't much chance of that leading anywhere. She wasn't from here, didn't intend to stay, and he wasn't going to leave. Still, a few days in Rae's company might nudge him out of the mopes he'd been wallowing in lately. It couldn't hurt; that was for sure. He pressed down on the accelerator as he pulled onto the state highway.

The diner was always busy on Saturdays, and he felt fortunate to find an empty booth. He quickly slid into one of the seats just as Dee plunked a cup of black coffee in front of him and handed him a menu. His good friend appeared a little frazzled for so early in the day.

"Hi, Dee, you shorthanded again?" Luke took the menu in case Rae needed it when she got there, but as often as he ate here, he could probably recite it for her word for word.

"Seems to be a way of life lately," she answered with a deep sigh. "Pancakes, bacon, and eggs, right?"

"You got it, but there's no hurry. I'm meeting Michael and his daughter here. I'll wait for them."

"Okay. I'll be back when they get here." Dee was already on her way to another table.

Luke took a sip of the hot liquid and took in his surroundings. Usually there was another waitress out front, with one cook in the back, and Dee helping out wherever needed. Today, there was just Dee and Charlie, and Luke understood she didn't have time for the usual small talk. He just wished she didn't have to work so hard. As far as he knew, Dee didn't have a personal life. There was a time, several years ago, he'd hoped that she and John, his cousin, would get together, but it never happened. He'd always thought it was a shame. They seemed to bring out a unique side in each other.

Luke shook his head. Here he was trying to play matchmaker, like he had any experience at it. He didn't even have a love of his own. Still, he thought Dee and John would have made a great couple.

He gazed out the window just in time to see Michael and Rae pull up outside. She seemed happier this morning. . .and very pretty. Her hair curled softly around her face, and she was smiling up at Michael as she followed him into the diner.

Luke stood when Michael waved from across the room and propelled his daughter ahead of him. "Good morning, Luke! It's a beautiful day, isn't it?"

"Good morning. It is a great day." Luke found it hard to take his gaze off of Rae. She was even prettier close-up. Her cheeks were rosy from the brisk morning air, and her blue eyes seemed to sparkle. "You seem well rested today. When Michael called about meeting you this morning, I was a little afraid he'd pulled you out of bed."

"Actually, I almost had to do that when she was in school." Michael chuckled. "But she surprised me by already having the coffee going when I got up this morning."

"I do feel rested, thank you." Rae arched an eyebrow at her dad and gave Luke a smile before sliding into the corner of the booth. Michael slid in beside her, and Luke took his seat once more. Rae faced her dad. "I am an adult now, you know."

Michael kissed her on the temple. "I know. Sometimes I wish you were still a kid, though."

"Sometimes I do too." Rae took the menu Luke pushed toward her. "What's good? I'm kind of hungry."

"Everything here is good, so just take your pick," Michael answered, glancing around the diner. "Dee seems a little short on help again today."

"I am," Dee confirmed, coming up behind him. "I haven't been able to get in touch with Nelda," she said, then glanced at Rae. "She's my regular waitress. She went out of town for a few days, but she was supposed to be back yesterday."

The door opened, and two more customers came in. Dee grinned. "Can't complain about business, though. Since you're regulars here and know me, I'll skip the small talk. Just give me your order fast as you can, and I'll get it out to you as soon as I can."

"I'll have the big breakfast special and coffee," Michael said. "With the eggs over easy."

"And I'll have the same thing, only with scrambled eggs," Rae added quickly.

Dee pointed at Luke. "I have your order, right?"

"You do."

She nodded and rushed off to another table.

"Poor thing. I hope she gets some help soon." Rae watched Dee take an order from another table.

"And I hope you can eat that breakfast you ordered, Rae," her dad teased. "It's a big one."

Luke laughed. "I was thinking the same thing."

"I just didn't want to take up her time by trying to make up my mind, Dad. What exactly did I order?"

"Three eggs, bacon and sausage, and a stack of pancakes this high." Luke grinned and motioned with his hands to show her just how high that stack was.

"Oh, no." Rae giggled and shook her head.

"With hash browns on the side," Michael added.

"Oh, well." She shrugged. "I'll share."

Dee returned with a pot of coffee and two cups. She poured their cups and set the pot down. "Hope you don't mind; I'll let you warm yours up, Luke."

Before he had a chance to answer, she spun off in another direction.

"Is it always this busy?" Rae asked.

"No. Good thing she's closed on Sundays. She's going to need the rest." Luke warmed his coffee from the pot Dee had left and took a drink.

"What is on the agenda today? Are you going to introduce Rae to Ellie and some of the rest of the family?" Michael asked.

"If she's game. I thought I'd show her around town and introduce her to Gram, and maybe to Jake and Sara too."

"Who is Ellie?" Rae glanced from her dad to Luke.

"She's my grandmother. A real jewel, if I do say so myself."

"She is that. Ellie is the grandmother everyone wishes was theirs," Michael stated.

Dee brought their breakfast just then, and the two men watched Rae's reaction at seeing the pile of food set before her. Luke laughed when she let out a deep breath and picked up her fork as if preparing for battle.

✍

Her dad left them at Luke's pickup, after exacting a promise from them to meet him back at the diner for lunch. They agreed, but if the truth be known, Rae didn't think she could ever eat again.

Luke opened the door for her and helped her into his truck before coming around and taking his seat behind the wheel. He glanced over at her and grinned. "If you want to walk some of that off before we come back, it's fine with me. My usual breakfast at home is a bowl of cereal."

Rae chuckled and wondered if he could read her mind. "I usually have a piece of toast. But it smelled so good when we walked in, I just had to indulge. Do you breakfast there often?"

"More than I should but not every day. And when I do, I don't usually stop for lunch."

"We can call Dad later and tell him we won't be there," Rae suggested, buckling her seat belt.

"No. He's looking forward to seeing you. And I can always just order a salad or soup."

"Good idea. That's what I'll do too."

Luke backed out of the parking space and headed the truck down the street. "I'll drive you out to see where Aunt Nora lives and then a little later we'll head over to Gram's. Your dad is a great favorite of hers, and I know she'd love to meet you."

Rae wasn't much interested in where Nora lived, but she couldn't say that to the woman's handsome nephew. He looked even better this morning than he had last night. She liked his slow grin and the way he leaned his head to the side when he talked to her. But he was Nora's kin, and she'd best keep that in mind. Somehow she didn't think she'd be spending the morning with this cowboy if his aunt hadn't had something to do with it.

"Is your grandmother Nora's mother?"

Luke shook his head. "No. Nora was married to Gram's son. But he died in Vietnam years ago."

"And she never remarried?" Somehow that surprised Rae. Nora was a very attractive woman.

"No, she never even showed any interest in another man until. . ." He pointed to a corner store. "That's our old-fashioned ice cream parlor. They also make some really good hot drinks in the winter."

Rae was sure he'd cut his sentence short on purpose. She was certain she had an idea of what he'd been about to say . . .that Nora hadn't shown any interest in another man until her dad came along. But she chose not to press the point. "I'll have to get in there for a cappuccino or hot chocolate while I'm here."

Luke kept pointing out different businesses while they drove down the street. There was the grocery store, several clothing stores, and the drugstore.

"It's quaint, all right," she said. "But I don't see myself ever living in a place like this. I just can't understand why my dad would want to live here. He always seemed to love Albuquerque."

Luke glanced over at her. "Well, I'm not going to pretend that we can compete with your Albuquerque, but the downtown area isn't all there is to Sweet Springs. There's the mall just off the highway and all kinds of chain restaurants and motels out there. There's an eight-screen movie theater that just opened up too. We have a really good Chinese restaurant and one of the best Mexican restaurants in the state down the road a piece. But I don't think it's what the town has to offer as far as places to go that attracted your dad."

"No? What is it then?" *Besides your aunt, that is,* Rae wanted to add, but instead, she waited for Luke's answer.

"I think it's the people and maybe the slower pace of life. Maybe he wanted to slow down and enjoy life a little."

Rae shrugged. She'd never thought about that. "Maybe. He just always seemed to thrive at home."

"Well, watch him close. I think maybe you'll find him thriving just fine here."

Rae wondered at the defensive tone in his voice. Had she insulted him? "Luke. . .I'm not putting Sweet Springs down. I'll admit it's a pretty little town. I'm just a city girl, I guess. I've never lived anywhere else. I didn't mean to upset you."

Luke shook his head. "I know you didn't. I guess I'm just a small-town guy. Let's see how you feel about wide-open spaces." He shifted gears as they headed out onto the highway.

Rae had to admit the area was pretty. Apple orchards climbed the hillside, and the sun gave the Hondo River in the valley an extra sparkle. The scenery could have been right out of a postcard. . .and that's the only place she'd ever seen anything like it. Could she help it if she felt more comfortable in city surroundings?

Luke showed her the turnoff to Nora's ranch, but the house couldn't be seen from the road. A few more miles passed before he turned off the highway. "This and Nora's land are both part of the same ranch, the T-Bar. Uncle Ben and Aunt Lydia live on down the road. The ranch is the family business, 'cept that my brother, Jake, and my cousin, John, are both lawyers. Several of the female cousins moved away and have businesses of their own. But the ranch has been in the family since Great-Great-Grandpa Tanner settled here. I live in the first ranch house built here. . .want to see it?"

"Sure, I'd love to." Rae was interested in seeing where Luke lived—and very curious now to see where this ranch and family had started here in New Mexico. She couldn't claim to be a native New Mexican. She'd been born in Oklahoma, as were her parents, but they'd moved to New Mexico when she was only two years old, and Albuquerque was the only home she'd known. She loved this state, and she would have loved to be able to claim that her family had helped settle the area. She took notice of the mountains in the distance. They might not be *her* mountain range. . .not as big and looming from here, but beautiful just the same.

The road curved, and finally she could see his house, a small two-story, standing in a grove of trees. Luke pulled up to it but didn't shut off the engine of the pickup.

"My family settled here back in the late 1800s—'bout 1881 from all accounts. The inside has been modernized, but on the outside it appears pretty much like it did back then."

Rae was surprised at how much she wanted to get out of the truck and see the inside of the house—learn a little more about the man beside her—but Luke backed out of the drive and headed toward the road again. Evidently he didn't want her seeing the inside of his home.

"Too bad you didn't get down here last month. The colors of the aspens were gorgeous."

"I wish I could have seen them," Rae said honestly. She loved the autumn colors. "Maybe next year I'll get down here. Albuquerque has its own colorful event in October too, you know."

Luke nodded. "I know. I've been there."

"To the balloon festival?"

"Yep. I've even gone up in a balloon. It sure is a sight to see. Both from the ground and from the air."

"Oh, wow. I've always wanted to do that, but I've never had the chance to go up in one."

"I have connections. Remind me next year, and I'll see what I can do about getting you a ride."

"Oh, with an offer like that, I'll be sure to."

The ride back to Sweet Springs seemed shorter than the one out to Luke's house, and Rae was almost disappointed when they pulled up at an older home in a residential section not far from the town square.

"Come on, it's time you met Gram." Luke cut off the engine.

Rae couldn't imagine why she felt so nervous about meeting Luke's grandmother, but she did. Was she a typical grandmother? Whatever that was. . . Rae wasn't sure she'd even know. She'd always longed for a large family with aunts and uncles and cousins, but both of her parents had been only children. They'd moved away from their families when she was a toddler. She could barely remember visits to see her grandparents on either side, and they'd all passed away when she was young. She and her dad were the Wellington family—what was left of it.

She walked beside Luke to the front door and was surprised when he opened it and walked in. No way would she leave her door unlocked in Albuquerque!

"Gram? You home?"

"Luke? Is that you? I'm here," a voice called. "Come on back to the kitchen."

Full as she still was, Rae's mouth began to water at the smells coming from the same direction as the voice. She followed Luke through the dining room into a large, sunny kitchen where an older woman stood at a large worktable, rolling out dough. She was of medium height and build, with short, silvery hair curling around her plump face. Her eyes were a bright blue behind her glasses, and her smile welcomed Rae.

"Well, who is this you've brought to meet me, Luke?" She brushed flour from her hands and wiped them on her apron before reaching out to shake Rae's hand.

"Gram, this is Rae Wellington, Michael's daughter. She's come for a visit, and he had to make rounds today. Rae, this is Ellie Tanner, my grandmother."

Rae was surprised when Luke's grandmother released her hand and enveloped her in a hug.

"Oh, how wonderful. We've all adopted Michael as family,

so that carries over to include you too, Dear. Welcome to Sweet Springs!"

"Thank you, Mrs. Tanner." Rae was at a loss for words. The warm welcome had unshed tears stinging the back of her throat. She hadn't expected to be so touched by this woman.

"Oh, please, just call me Ellie or Gram. Everyone else does. Sit down at the table and make yourselves at home. I'm just about to take my butternut pound cake out of the oven, and these pies can wait. Would you like a cup of coffee? Or I can put on a pot of tea—"

"Oh, no, thank you, Mrs.—uh, *Gram*. I'm still full from breakfast at the diner, and we have to meet Dad for lunch in a little while, although the smell of that cake is making my stomach growl as if I were starved." Rae grinned and rubbed her stomach in an effort to quiet it as she sat down at the table in the bay window.

"Well, I could use a cup of coffee about now." Luke got up to get himself a cup from the cabinet closest to the coffeepot. "That cake sure smells good, but I guess I'll wait until tomorrow night to have a piece. What kind of pies are you making?"

"Oh, apple and cherry, I guess."

"No pecan?"

Gram chuckled. "Luke, I'll be sure to double up for Thanksgiving, but no pecan for tomorrow night."

Luke joined Rae at the table. "Not even if I shell the nuts?"

"Not even then."

As Gram and Luke teased and talked, Rae listened, enjoying the lighthearted banter between the two. It was obvious that they loved each other.

She didn't know what kind of dinner was planned for the next night, but as she watched Gram take the cake from the oven, she definitely wished she could be there. Gram immediately transferred the tall, golden cake to a plate. It smelled delicious. For a minute Rae was tempted to ask for a piece.

Luke glanced at his watch and took a final drink from his cup. "Guess we'd better be heading back downtown. Michael will have the law out, thinking I might have abducted you."

"You be sure and come to Sunday night supper with Michael tomorrow night, Dear. You'll get to meet a lot more people that way."

"Oh, I'd love to!" Rae exclaimed, surprising herself. She smiled at Gram. "I'd been wondering how I could get a taste of that cake," she said, blushing at her own audacity.

"Well, I'll make sure you do," Luke assured her. He placed his hand at her back as they headed out of the kitchen. Gram followed them to the front door.

Luke's touch and his grandmother's welcome made Rae feel as if she belonged here, and for a moment she wished she did. She felt happier and more relaxed than she had in weeks. She loved the feeling of this house and was really looking forward to coming back to it. She spun back around and asked, "Is there anything I can help with, or bring, for tomorrow night?"

"You just bring yourself this time, Dear. I'll find something for you to do once you get here."

"Sounds wonderful. It was so nice to meet you, Gram." It just felt natural to call her that.

"You just stop in anytime, you hear?"

"Thank you. I might just do that."

Once in the pickup, Rae and Luke waved back at Gram, who was still waving from the doorway when they drove off.

Something in Rae wanted to run right back to Ellie Tanner's house, sit down, and pour out all her troubles to the grandmother she wished was her own.

four

After pointing out a few more businesses—the florist, the bakery, and another gift store, then passing by the hospital, Luke drove Rae back to the diner. He'd enjoyed the morning with her. He'd seen a sweetness in her at his grandmother's that he liked a lot—and would like to see more of. He didn't know exactly what she'd been through in the last year, but Rae seemed to begin to relax at Gram's, only to tense up again now, as they walked toward the booth where Michael and Nora waited for them.

It appeared Aunt Nora was right; Rae wasn't very happy about her dad and his aunt seeing each other.

Michael stood up to give his daughter a hug, and Luke waited until she'd slid to the far end of the booth before sitting down beside her. There was an expression in her eyes that had him wanting to assure her everything would be all right. At the same time, he wanted to say something similar to his aunt who seemed just as apprehensive as Rae. Maybe it was just a woman thing he didn't understand. Whatever it was made him decidedly uncomfortable.

Rae seemed to be trying as she smiled at her dad. "I met Luke's grandmother just a little while ago. She's really nice."

The tension seemed to break for a moment as Michael and Nora both grinned. "She is that. She's just. . .Gram. And I think the whole town feels that way," Michael said

"She's the glue that's held this family together in some tough times," Nora said. "And the one we all go to when we need straight talk or a hug."

"Gram asked me to come to Sunday night supper tomorrow.

And she had this scrumptious cake that I can't wait to try."

"Oh, good. I was hoping you'd want to go. Ellie's suppers have become a delightful routine I would hate to miss," Michael admitted.

"Do I need to bring anything? She told me I didn't, but. . ." Rae glanced from Michael to Nora.

"Don't worry about it, Rae. Some of us bring something extra, but there is always plenty of food," Nora assured her.

Dee showed up to take their orders just then, appearing a little less frazzled than she had that morning.

"I see you have more help now, Dee. Nelda must have made it in," Rae said.

Dee shook her head. "Actually, no, and my part-time help is sick. Charlie, one of my cooks, called in his sister. She works at the Mexican restaurant but was off today. She can only help out today, so if Nelda isn't back by Monday, I guess I'll have to try to hire someone to take her place. I'm just thankful to have the help today."

"Good, because I was about to offer to help. And I know nothing about being a waitress," Rae admitted.

Dee grinned at Rae. "I probably would have taken you up on it. And on-the-job training is the very best kind. Thank you for the thought."

"You're welcome."

They each placed their orders, with both Luke and Rae ordering salads.

Dee laughed knowingly. "Breakfast was too much for you?"

"You should put a postscript on the menu, telling only the starving to order it," Rae said and laughed. "Or maybe have a petite order of the same thing."

"Now *that's* an idea." Dee hurried off to put in their order.

"So, Honey, what do you think of Sweet Springs after seeing a bit of it?" Michael asked.

"It's kind of quaint, and there is more to the town than I

first thought. But it's not Albuquerque, Dad."

Luke's heart sank, and he wasn't sure why. Obviously, Rae wasn't likely to fall in love with the area that was so much a part of him.

"Exactly. Life is slower here. There's time to enjoy it."

Rae raised an eyebrow at Luke.

He shrugged, remembering their earlier conversation. "Michael never told me that. It was just a feeling I had."

"What are you two talking about?" Nora asked.

"We were talking earlier about why someone would like living here." Luke shrugged. "I suggested pretty much the same thing Michael just said, but we've never discussed it."

"Well, I guess I'm not ready for a slow pace." Rae shook her head.

"Slow pace? Oh, Honey, just come work here for awhile," Dee teased as she brought their orders. She grinned at Rae. "There is no slow pace in this diner."

"There goes your theory." Rae gently nudged Luke on the shoulder.

"Must be the people then." He grinned down at her. Their gazes met for a moment, and Rae's smile warmed his heart.

"Might be," she agreed.

Luke's heart skipped a beat before she broke eye contact and concentrated on putting salt and pepper on her salad. He gave his attention to his own plate while Michael and Nora concentrated on the food Dee set down in front of them, commenting on how good it looked. He was pretty sure he wasn't the only one at the table who was having a problem with knowing what to say next.

Michael seemed as confused as Luke felt, but the wink he gave Nora seemed to encourage her to strike up a conversation with Rae.

"Rae, your dad says you'll be here for a little while. . .that you've taken a leave of absence. You know we have an excellent school system here, should you decide you might want to move—"

Luke's pulse jumped. Was there a chance Rae would move here?

"Thank you, Nora, but I don't think—"

"Oh, Honey, don't make a decision right away," Michael said. "I know you plan on going back to Albuquerque, but keep an open mind until after the New Year, will you?"

"You're staying a few months?" Luke had thought she was only staying the weekend.

"I'm not sure exactly what I'm doing. I promised Dad I'd stay through this next week. After that, I don't know."

"Oh, Rae, you know you'd just be coming back for Thanksgiving and then again for Christmas."

"Unless I could talk you into coming up there."

"Honey—"

"I know, Dad. I'm just teasing. Even if I go back home, I'll be back for the holidays. I don't want to spend them alone."

Luke had never spent Thanksgiving or Christmas alone, and he sure didn't like the thought of it for anyone else—especially Rae.

"Sweet Springs decorates real pretty for Christmas. Be a shame to miss it."

"So does Albuquerque."

Luke nodded and chuckled. "I'm sure it does. I'll have to get up there one of these days."

"You should. Be a shame to miss it." The corners of Rae's mouth turned up in a broad grin as she teased him back. He had a feeling she enjoyed this kind of give-and-take as much as he did.

Luke glanced over to see Michael and his aunt watching them with interest. Nora cleared her throat and smiled. "I've seen the beautiful luminaries in Old Town. It is quite a treat. We have them around our town square too, but of course it's nothing like Albuquerque."

"I noticed some fall-like decorations around town. . .bales

of hay, a scarecrow here and there. It is quaint. Does the town pay for that or just the businesses?"

"A little of both. This is the first year they've decorated for anything besides Christmas. The town council just approved the funds for Thanksgiving and several other holidays. . .kind of a seasonal decorating." Luke motioned to his aunt. "Aunt Nora got it started. With all the building up out on the highway, we wanted to make sure that our little *old town* stays alive."

"There's a contest at Christmastime for the best decorated business downtown. Everyone seems to get involved in that," Nora said.

Dee came back to see if they needed anything, and it seemed to be a cue for the end of the lunch break.

"Rae and I have to go to the store to pick up a few things for supper. I'm grilling steaks tonight, Luke. Nora is coming, and we'd love to have you join us if you can," Michael offered. Luke stood up to let Rae stand, noting that she seemed overly busy scooting out of the booth. She seemed to be trying to ignore him, and when she didn't echo her dad's invitation, he was left with the impression she'd seen enough of him for one day.

"Thanks, Michael, but Aunt Lydia invited me to eat supper over there. Uncle Ben and I have some business to go over."

"Maybe another time, then." Michael grabbed the ticket Deana tore off her pad. "Lunch is on me today."

"There's no need—"

"Yes there is. Rae and I appreciate you showing her around today." Michael gazed down at Nora. "Are you leaving now too?"

She shook her head. "I've got a beauty shop appointment in about thirty minutes; I think I'll have another cup of coffee before I go. How about keeping me company, Luke?"

He had a feeling his aunt wanted to find out how the

morning went. He might as well stay. Nora wouldn't rest until he gave her a full report.

"Sure, I'll have a second cup of coffee."

Luke felt a light touch on his jacket sleeve, and he gazed down into Rae's eyes. "Thank you for showing me around and introducing me to Gram. I'm looking forward to seeing her again."

"You're welcome. Thanks for keeping me company this morning. Y'all have a good evening." Luke took his seat across from Nora once more.

Michael joined Rae back at the table. "See you about six, Nora?"

"I'll be there. Can I bring anything?"

"Just yourself. Rae and I will take care of the rest."

A glance passed between the two that was so full of love, Luke felt he was intruding. He glanced away and saw the expression on Rae's face as she watched them. No, she still wasn't happy about Nora and Michael's relationship.

Michael gave a quick wave as he and Rae left the diner. Luke took a drink from his cup, waiting for Nora to start pelting him with questions. She had a dreamy expression in her eyes, and it took a moment before she seemed to realize where she was. No doubt about it—Nora was in love.

"Luke, how did your morning go? Rae seems nice."

That was it? He'd figured on all kinds of questions from his aunt. "It went fine. And she is very nice." *And pretty, and she smells good.*

Nora sighed. "But she still doesn't like me."

"We didn't talk about you, Aunt Nora."

"Probably because I'm your aunt. It's all right, though. Michael and I talked, and he assured me things will work out."

"He thinks there's a problem?"

"Well, she was a little upset that he hadn't told her about me. And I can understand that. He should have. But he's assured me she'll come around—and that he's not giving me up even if she doesn't."

"Well, see? There's nothing to worry about, then."

"It will just be so much better if she'll accept me. Will you pray that she will, Luke? I don't want to cause a rift between father and daughter."

Luke reached over and patted his aunt's hand. "Of course I will, Aunt Nora. And I think Rae will come around too; I really do."

Surely she would. Nora and Michael made each other happy. Rae was bound to see that. But he'd pray anyway. It could only help.

&

Rae and her dad stopped at the grocery store to pick up three steaks to grill that night. She tried not to show her disappointment that Nora was invited. Rae wished Luke had accepted her dad's invitation to dinner, but she hadn't wanted him to feel pressured, so she'd just kept her mouth shut. Besides, he'd probably had enough of her company for one day. She had enjoyed his company more than she'd anticipated. He was different than she thought he would be. Somehow she'd expected him to be a little cocky, but he wasn't. He didn't seem to have to try to make an impression. He was who he was and seemed very comfortable with that.

Once they got home, her dad made up a marinade for the meat while she washed potatoes and wrapped them in foil to bake. "I'll make the salad just before we eat, Dad."

"Thanks, Honey. It's so good to have you here. I do hope you'll stay as long as you want."

"I'll probably stay." She sighed. "I love Albuquerque, but it doesn't feel the same now. I don't know why, exactly. It never used to have a lonely feel to it, but now it does."

He rubbed his chin. "I know. I've felt the same way."

"Is that why you moved?"

"Partly. I missed your mother, and. . .I thought you had a new life starting with Paul."

"So did I. Guess we were both wrong. Dad, how could I have misread him so badly?"

"Honey, don't blame yourself. I liked Paul. He fooled me too."

It didn't hurt so much to talk about him tonight, and suddenly Rae realized that she hadn't thought of Paul all day. Not once that she could remember—until her dad mentioned him. She wanted to get over the breakup, but she certainly wasn't ready for another man to occupy her thoughts in Paul's place!

"I'm just glad you found out what he's like before you married him, Honey. He wouldn't have been faithful. But the Lord will send someone into your life who will love you the way he should. I'm sure of it."

"I hope so, Dad. But right now there's not a man on this planet I could trust except you. I think it will be a long time before I'm ready to give my heart to anyone else."

She enjoyed the rest of the afternoon with her dad, puttering around in the kitchen and hearing about how much his medical practice was growing. She was pleased that supper with Nora went smoother than she expected it to, although she was very relieved when they shooed Rae out of the kitchen and did the dishes.

She jumped at the chance to go to her room. "I think I'll call it a night, if y'all don't mind. I haven't had a chance to unpack and get settled in."

"You go right ahead, Honey. Does the 'settle in' part mean you're going to stay through the holidays?"

"I'm not sure, Dad. I'm thinking about it, okay?"

She was relieved when he didn't press the issue. "Okay. Do you want me to wake you in time for church tomorrow?"

"What time does it start?"

"Sunday school is at nine-thirty, church at ten-thirty. I usually go to both."

"I'll set my alarm and go with you, then." She kissed him on the cheek and smiled at Nora. "Night, Nora. I guess I'll see you at church tomorrow?"

"You will. Hope you sleep well, Rae."

"Thanks. Good night, Dad." Rae headed down the hall to her room, glad to be able to get away. The last thing she wanted to do was intercept any more of the loving gazes they'd given each other at Deana's.

Since she wasn't ready for bed, she ended up out on the patio, curled up in a deck chair and gazing up at the starlit sky. She wondered if Luke was at his aunt and uncle's. It really had been nice of him to show her around and introduce her to his grandmother. Rae was sure he could have found all kinds of things to do besides spending his morning with her. She couldn't help wondering if he was seeing someone. She'd pretty much decided it wasn't Dee. They just seemed to be very good friends. But he was so nice and so handsome; there must be *someone* he was seeing.

She heard a burst of laughter and twisted around to see her dad and Nora through the kitchen window as they cleaned up. He was laughing at something Nora said, and then he gave her a quick kiss on her nose. He was happy. And Rae wished she could be happy for him.

But she was jealous. . .and she didn't know if it was because Nora had so much of her dad's attention, or if it was because they seemed to have such a good relationship while hers and Paul's had crumbled. And she just couldn't make herself like Nora. How was she ever going to accept her?

Not wanting the couple to look out and think she was spying on them, she hurried back to her room. She didn't know if she could handle feeling like a fifth wheel around here until after the New Year.

❧

Luke enjoyed having supper and visiting with his aunt and uncle. He had a wonderful family. When his and Jake's parents had been killed in wreck all those years ago, his grandparents took the boys in and raised them, but Aunt Lydia and Uncle Ben had been there too. They'd given him and Jake their support, cheered for their baseball and football games, and advised them when needed. Their son, John, was more like a brother than a cousin. Luke loved them just as much as he loved Gram. Now, as he sat at the kitchen table with a piece of his aunt's peach cobbler and a cup of coffee in front of him, he sent up a prayer of thanksgiving that the Lord had seen fit to provide him with the love and support of this family.

"Nora told us that Michael's daughter is in town," Lydia said.

"She is. I almost brought her out here today. I was showing her around while Michael made rounds this morning."

"Oh?" His aunt joined him and Ben at the table.

"Don't read anything into that, Aunt Lydia. I was doing it for Aunt Nora. Besides, Rae is a city girl. I can't quite see her leaving Albuquerque for Sweet Springs."

"Well, stranger things have happened. What about Jake? He came back."

"Yes, but his roots were here. Rae's aren't."

"Well, what's she like?" his uncle asked.

"Real pretty. Real nice but kind of sad." It was true, Luke realized as soon as the words were out of his mouth. She was all of those things. . .and a bit irritating with her city-girl view of Sweet Springs. He'd had to pray not to lose his temper this morning as he showed her around. She didn't like his town, the area, or the fact that her father had moved here. Luke didn't think anything he showed her was likely to change her mind. Still, he hadn't wanted to add to the deep sadness he'd seen in her eyes. He couldn't help wondering why it was there, and he wished he'd asked Nora more about her. Surely she had an idea what it was Michael was talking about when he mentioned that things had been hard on Rae.

"Hmm, wonder why," Lydia mused.

"I don't know." But he intended to find out. Maybe it was that sadness that reached out to him. There was something about Rae Wellington that had him wanting to fix whatever it was that was wrong in her life. And somehow he just didn't think it was only about Aunt Nora.

"Nora is a little worried she won't accept her." Lydia took a sip from her cup.

"I'm sure she'll come around," Luke assured his aunt. "Besides, Michael and Aunt Nora are meant for each other."

Hoping to get Michael's daughter off his mind and to keep from having to answer more questions, he changed the subject. "How's John doing up in Santa Fe? Has he decided to run for senator for sure?"

"He says the backing is there. He's says he'll make up his mind in the next week or so."

The rest of the evening was spent discussing the pros and cons of his cousin's possible run for United States senator. As much as the family would miss John if he had to move to Washington, D.C., they all were convinced that he would make a wonderful senator.

At least talking about John's chances kept his mind off of Rae Wellington. . .for a little while.

❧

The next morning, Rae followed Dad down the aisle of the small church he attended. She'd already met and been warmly greeted by what was surely at least half the congregation. That they loved her dad was obvious, and she could see he felt the same about them.

As welcome as everyone tried to make her feel, she was still a little uncomfortable. Probably because she hadn't been attending church at home like she should have ever since the breakup with Paul.

As they took seats on a pew behind Luke, Gram, and several others she presumed to be more family, she felt even more welcomed. There was a couple about her age with a toddler, and an older man sat by Gram. It felt good to be there, even though she didn't much like the fact that Nora sat on the other side of her dad. She tried not to show it as she greeted the other woman.

"Good morning, Nora. How are you today?"

"Just fine. You look lovely, Rae," Nora said.

"Thank you,; so do you." Nora looked beautiful in the deep-rose-colored suit she wore. Rae was glad she'd packed her favorite cream-colored suit and teal blouse, because she always felt confident and at ease in the outfit.

Gram glanced over her shoulder and asked, "You are coming tonight, aren't you?"

"We wouldn't miss it," Dad answered with a smile.

Sunday school started with a prayer, and Rae bowed her head. Tears sprung to her eyes as she realized how badly she'd missed praying and talking to the Lord. She enjoyed the Bible class and the worship service that followed more than she thought she would. The minister was a fairly young man—probably in his late thirties—and his sermon about God's love and grace touched her heart. She might be a stranger in town, but by the end of the service, her soul felt as if it had come home.

She'd wanted to talk to Luke after worship services, but so many people crowded around them that when she finally located him, he was already making his way out the door.

The rest of the day sped by. Dad took her and Nora to lunch at the Italian restaurant Luke had pointed out the day before. She enjoyed the atmosphere and the meal. But hard as she told herself she was trying to graciously share him with Nora, she wished she had her dad to herself. She didn't like the way the woman seemed to be trying so hard to make friends with her. Just because her dad was seeing Nora, it didn't mean the women had to be buddies, did it?

After lunch Dad took them for a Sunday drive so that Rae would know her way around better when he had to go to work the next day.

"We could go to the ice cream parlor for dessert," he suggested.

"Oh, Rae, they make the most wonderful hot fudge sundaes," Nora added, turning to her with a smile.

"No, thanks." Rae shook her head. "None for me, but why don't you two go? I want to make some cookies to take to Gram's tonight."

"You don't have to do that, Dear. There will be plenty of food there," Nora assured her.

"I'm sure there will be. But I just don't feel right going empty-handed." And she didn't want to spend the rest of the afternoon with Nora and her dad.

"All right, Honey." Her dad looked at her through the rearview mirror. "I'll take you home so you can make your cookies, and Nora and I will go out for dessert so we don't snitch your delicious cookies before they can cool," he teased.

If her dad suspected that she just wanted some time to herself, he didn't give her away. Rae breathed a sigh of relief and waved to them when they dropped her off at home and headed back to town. Glad that she'd been able to cut the afternoon with Nora short, she hurried inside, preheated the oven, and went to change clothes. Rae mixed the brown sugar, eggs, flour, and flavoring, idly wondering if Luke would be at his grandmother's tonight. She'd tried to quit thinking about how handsome he was in that navy suit, crisp white shirt, and red tie that morning, but it just wasn't working very well. She'd been thinking of him off and on all afternoon, and she couldn't deny that she hoped he'd show up at his grandmother's for supper.

Immediately after church services, that night they headed over to Gram's. Rae didn't realize just how much she'd been watching for Luke until she glanced up to see him crossing the room toward her. Her heartbeat felt totally confused, coming to a stop and then going into overdrive when Luke smiled at her. She hoped no one could tell how flustered she was.

He brought his brother, Jake, sister-in-law, Sara, and their toddler, Meggie, over to meet her. They'd been the couple sitting on the pew with Luke and Gram that morning. A bond seemed to form between her and Sara once they found out they were both teachers, even though neither was actively teaching at the moment. Before long, they'd made plans to get together in the coming week, and Rae was really looking forward to it.

If she thought she'd met half the church congregation that morning, Rae was sure she met the other half that night. Luke kept her busy meeting other family members and friends. She liked the way his hand lightly touched her back, guiding her from one group of people to another. It made her feel watched over and special. He stayed at her side most of the evening, seeming to have taken it as his responsibility to introduce her to everyone.

There was William Oliver, Sara's dad, who'd been sitting beside Gram in church that morning. Rae found out the older couple was seeing each other and the family was hoping they would marry. She also met Luke's Aunt Lydia and Uncle Ben—a lovely couple who told her how happy they were to meet Michael's daughter. They invited her to come out and visit anytime while she was here.

Before the evening was over, Rae felt she must have met everyone there, thanks to Luke, and she had a glimpse of what a large family was like. She could almost see what her dad's attraction to Nora was—she belonged to this wonderful family.

five

Luke woke Monday morning feeling a little grouchy. While he'd spent the evening before at Rae's side, he hadn't really had a chance to talk to her. He couldn't figure out why it bothered him so much, but it did. He was attracted to her—there was no doubt in his mind about that. Luke sighed and reminded himself he'd be better off steering clear of the city girl. Only that's not what he wanted to do.

She was sweet. She'd been so nice to everyone he'd introduced her to; he could tell his whole family had really liked her. So did he—in spite of warning himself not to.

He spent most of the morning in his office catching up on paperwork and checking in with the ranch foremen in other parts of the state. Sometimes he missed just being out on the land, but Uncle Ben had been handling things for a lot of years. He deserved a retirement before he was too old to enjoy it. Besides, if John did run for the senate, Ben and Lydia would be out on the campaign trail right along with him.

Luke made sure his cell phone had a good charge before heading into town to Jake's office to sign a contract selling off some beef. Maybe then he could check in on Rae and see how she was doing. He could offer to show her around some more, maybe offer to buy her lunch. He punched in the numbers to Michael's home phone and waited for Rae to pick up. But he got the answering machine instead.

He wondered if she'd gone back to Albuquerque, and he acknowledged to himself that he'd be disappointed if she did. In fact, deep inside he wanted to get to know her better.

He stopped at the diner, thinking Rae might have gone

there for breakfast, but she hadn't. Seeing how busy Dee was, he decided she didn't need his business that badly this morning. He could get a cup of coffee at the law office.

Nancy, the law firm's secretary, smiled and waved him into Jake's office, where his brother was poring over a pile of papers on his desk. He glanced up over the reading glasses perched on his nose. Luke chuckled at the picture he made, knowing Jake wasn't happy about having to finally give in and wear glasses.

"You're a sight, you are," Luke said, crossing the room to pour a cup of coffee.

"And you are a pain, little brother."

"Got those papers ready for me to sign?"

Jake ruffled through some files on his desk until he found what he was hunting for. He glanced inside and nodded. "They're all here. I didn't expect you until this afternoon. What brings you into town early today?"

"I just thought I'd just come pester you a little while."

Jake grinned and glanced out of the window. "Right. I thought it might be Michael's daughter. I saw her going in and out of several shops earlier. Thought maybe you were going to meet her for lunch."

Luke set his cup down on Jake's desk and glanced out the window. "You did? How long ago?"

Jake shrugged his shoulders and grinned. "About a half hour or so ago. She's probably still out there somewhere."

Luke knew his brother. He was trying to find out more than Luke was ready to tell him at the moment. He eased down in the chair across from Jake and picked up his cup. "Guess she's going to stay awhile after all."

"You could probably catch her if you hurry." Jake rocked back in his chair.

Luke leaned back in his. "I came here to sign some papers, Brother. Let's get at them."

Jake chuckled and opened the file. He pulled out a stack of

papers and pushed them toward Luke. "Here they are. Just sign on those bottom lines. If you hurry, I'll treat you to lunch before my one o'clock appointment."

"You've got a deal." Luke started signing.

They were just about to walk out of the door of Jake's office when Nancy told him Sara was on the phone.

"Go on over and grab us a table. I'll be there in a few minutes," Jake said, then walked back to his desk and picked up the phone. "Hi, Darlin'. What's up?"

Luke waved and headed out the door. Jake's tone of voice always changed when he talked to Sara. He was so glad those two had found each other again—even if he did feel like a fifth wheel around the two of them half the time.

He walked out onto the sidewalk and headed for the diner. He just hoped there was an empty table.

❧

Rae woke to total quiet and glanced at the clock on her nightstand. Nine o'clock! Why hadn't her dad awakened her before he went on rounds? She threw back the covers, pulled on her robe, and hurried to the kitchen.

There she found a note propped up against the coffeepot. *Rae, I had an emergency at the hospital. Didn't want to wake you. If you can, meet me at the diner for lunch. Unless you call my office and let me know otherwise, I'll meet you there around noon.*

Rae was sure she could find her way back to the diner. Maybe she'd get ready early and explore a couple of the shops Luke had pointed out to her on Saturday. It wouldn't take long, and then she could meet her dad for lunch.

She poured a cup of coffee and made herself a piece of toast before heading for the shower.

A couple of hours later, she was downtown and finding that there was much more to see than she'd first imagined. Along the side streets there were several blocks of businesses, including several really nice gift shops, a couple of craft stores, and a jewelry store specializing in turquoise. She'd spotted the library on the other side of the square and made note to stop and pick out a few books before she went home. All in all, she had a delightful morning and was beginning to get hungry. She checked her watch and realized she'd better hurry if she was going to meet her dad on time. She rounded the corner and stepped straight into the arms of Luke Breland.

He reached out to steady her. "Whoa! Rae, I called you earlier to see if you might want to meet for a bite to eat. When I got the answering machine, I thought maybe you'd gone back to your mountains."

Rae took a minute to regain her balance and try to will her heart out of overdrive. She'd been trying *not* to think about this tall cowboy all morning. Now here she was—with his arms almost encircling her—gazing up into those beautiful brown eyes of his. Out in the sunshine they reminded her of melted chocolate, all shiny and warm.

"I'm sorry. I wasn't watching where I was going. I'm supposed to be meeting Dad for lunch, but I lost track of time."

"Found more to do than you thought you would, huh?" Luke grinned at her.

She smiled at him and conceded, "I found a few things of interest. Where are you headed?"

"Same place you are. Jake is meeting me for lunch. . .after he gets off the phone with Sara."

"They are so nice. I enjoyed meeting them last night." Rae liked the way Luke grasped her elbow as they crossed the street and entered the diner.

Luke canvassed the area from over her head. "There is only one table open. I don't see your dad here yet. Do you think he would mind sharing with Jake and me?"

"I'm sure he wouldn't. Let's grab it before we lose it," Rae suggested as the door behind them opened to three more people.

She and Luke hurried over to the table and sat down just as Dee dropped two menus on the table. "Be back in a few minutes."

Rae couldn't see anyone else waiting tables. By all appearances Dee was shorthanded again this week. She breathed a sigh of relief for Dee when two couples paid for their meals and left—only to be replaced by people waiting at the door. Her dad walked in with Jake, and she waved them over.

"I thought I saw you shopping earlier today, Rae," Jake said as he took a seat and raised an eyebrow at his brother. "Sara really enjoyed meeting you last night. She'd like to have you over for dinner while you're here."

"Oh, how nice. I'd like that." She really would like to get to know the couple better.

Dee ran back over to take their order and let out a huge sigh as she flipped her order pad to a clean page.

"I see you didn't get ahold of Nelda," Luke stated.

"Actually, her daughter called me—the poor kid sounded really frazzled. She apologized for not letting me know sooner that Nelda was in a car accident and has been in the hospital. She broke her leg and will be recuperating at her daughter's. It will be at least six weeks before she's out of the cast. And there will be physical therapy after that. Keep her in your prayers, okay? I'm going to call the paper this afternoon to place an ad for some help."

She gave them an overly bright smile before she continued. "Hope you all are having a better day than I am. What can I get you?"

At that news, it was as if everyone at the table silently agreed to make it easy on her. They all ordered the daily special.

"I don't think I've ever seen it so busy in here," Jake said as Dee rushed off to put in their order. "But I don't think she'd want us to go somewhere else."

"No, she wouldn't." Luke shook his head. "I think it just

seems busier because Dee is so shorthanded and can't get to everyone as fast as usual. Thankfully, everyone seems to be taking the delay in getting their food graciously."

He was right. All of Dee's patrons did seem to be taking the slower service in stride. But watching her race from one customer to another and back and forth from the service window to give orders to her cook, Rae's sympathies were with Dee.

Charlie certainly was holding up his end, getting out orders as fast as he could, but Dee was beginning to appear a little frazzled herself. By the time Rae had finished her meal, she just couldn't take it anymore.

When Dee stopped at the table to refill her glass of iced tea, Rae stood up. "Do you have an apron and another order pad and pencil?"

"You serious?"

"If you don't mind training me on the job."

"Are you kidding? I told you that's the best kind of training." She whirled back to the service window and shouted, "Charlie, throw out a clean apron. Help is on the way!"

"You sure about this, Rae?" Dad asked.

"I just can't sit here another minute and watch Dee. I'm getting dizzy. Besides, you have to go back to work, and I need something to do—especially if I'm going to stay until after the holidays. There are presents to buy, you know."

"If it means you're staying awhile, then I'm all for it. Go to work, Girl."

"It's a good thing you're doing, Rae." Luke's gaze met hers. "I was seriously thinking about volunteering, myself."

"Yeah, right." Jake shook his head and laughed. "I can see you with that apron on."

Rae ignored their chuckles as she followed Dee to the kitchen door.

"God bless you, Rae." Dee handed her a fresh order pad

and the apron Charlie had given her. She helped Rae tie it in back. "I can't thank you enough."

"You may not say that in an hour or two. I really don't know what I'm doing," Rae admitted as Dee handed her a pencil.

"At this point, just getting menus and water to customers until I can get to them would be a big help."

"Well, I think I can handle that. . .maybe a little more than that. Where do you want me to start?"

"You take care of the counter here surrounding the service window. That way you can ask Charlie questions if you need to. I'll take care of the booths and tables."

"Okay. How about I see if any of these customers need anything else? Do you have their tickets?"

"Oh, you are going to work out just fine if you're concerned about me getting my money." Dee grinned at her. "I'll give them their bills. Do you know how to run a cash register?"

"I do. I worked in a bookstore while I was going to college. This doesn't seem that different."

Dee nodded. "Okay. Just ask if you have any questions. Thanks again, Rae."

≈

"That was nice of Rae, Michael." Luke motioned in the direction of Dee and Rae as they stood in the center of the counter area. Rae had surprised him by offering to help Dee. "Has she ever done this kind of work before?"

Michael shook his head. "No, but she's always had a mind of her own, and she's not afraid of hard work." He glanced at his watch and pushed back his chair. "I'd better get back to my office."

Jake stood and took one last drink of water. "Yeah. I was thinking the same thing. You coming, Luke?"

"Huh? Oh, yeah. I need to get back to the ranch. I'll walk back to your office with you."

They all headed to the register at the same time, apparently to Rae's relief. "Oh, good. I can practice on y'all."

"And you'd better not charge us a penny too much," Michael teased.

"There's no charge for yours, Rae." Dee came up behind her. "Least I can do is feed you."

"Thanks."

Luke watched as Rae concentrated on ringing up her dad's ticket. She seemed a little nervous as Dee looked on. Her sigh was audible when Dee assured her, "You did just fine. You don't need my supervision on this."

Dee patted her on the back and went to pick up an order Charlie had just placed in the service window.

Rae rang up Jake and Luke's ticket and grinned as she gave Jake his change. In an exaggerated drawl, she said, "Y'all come on back to see us, okay?"

Luke didn't know what to make of *this* Rae. She seemed to be coming out of her shell right before his eyes.

"You can count on it," Jake answered for Luke. They headed out the door, but Luke took one last glance back as she greeted a new customer with a smile. She sure was cute.

They parted at Jake's office. "Why don't you come over for supper tonight, Luke? You know Sara always makes plenty of food."

"I'll take a rain check, thanks."

"Ahh. Going to eat at the diner, are you?"

"I might."

Jake stopped at the door. "I thought so. Seems she's going to stay awhile. Sara wants to have her to dinner one night soon."

"Well, when you do—"

"Yeah?"

"I'll use that rain check."

Jake chuckled and slapped Luke on the back. "Somehow, I thought you would."

◦◦

The afternoon flew by as Rae learned the ropes of being a good waitress. She'd just cleaned off a table and taken the dishes back to the kitchen when Dee called her out front. There were only a few people left, and Dee was just pouring two glasses of iced tea.

"There is light at the end of the tunnel. Come take a break." Rae took a seat at one end of the counter, and Dee handed her a glass.

Rae hadn't realized how thirsty she was until she drained half the glass in almost one swallow. "Oh, that's good. Thank you."

"No. Thank *you*." Dee took a seat next to her. "I really appreciate your help today. With Nelda down, and Jen, my part-time helper, out sick with a cold, I was beginning to cave. Having you here really made a big difference."

"I'm glad. It's been fun, actually. I can help you out until after Christmas if you want. Maybe by then Nelda will be able to come back."

"Are you sure? It would be great if you really want to. I kind of hate to hire someone knowing it'd only be until Nelda comes back. It doesn't seem quite fair if they need a permanent job."

"I'm sure. I've been wondering what I was going to do all day with Dad at work."

"Well, I'm not going to turn your offer down. Just let me know what hours you want to work."

"Whatever works best for you. It seems you need help mostly during the rush times morning, noon, and night."

"I do, but no one wants to come and go. Split shifts are tough."

Rae shrugged. "I don't mind. Just work out a schedule for me, and I'll be here."

Joe, the cook who had relieved Charlie, peeked through

the service window. "I think God has answered your prayers, Dee. I'd get to makin' that schedule if I was you."

Dee hopped off the counter stool. "I'm not even going to ask a second time if she's sure, Joe. I'm going to make out that schedule right now."

Rae watched her hurry to the back and smiled. Dee didn't need to worry. She wasn't going to change her mind. It felt good to be helping someone out. She rang up the last customer and brought out clean glasses and cups from the back. No wonder Dee was so slim. There was always something to do here.

The kitchen smelled wonderful. Joe was stirring a big pot of spaghetti sauce that would be part of the dinner special. Rae had been relieved to find that Dee employed two cooks, and both of them were in good health. It had to be hard to run a place like this when people called in sick. Small though it was, when full, the diner could easily keep everyone hopping to keep up.

Dee came back in from her office and handed Rae a schedule. "Will this work for you?"

Rae glanced at it and nodded. Dee had her working only three times a week and for only six-hour shifts. Rae wouldn't have minded a few more days. She was going to be a little at loose ends during the day, and she had a feeling she was going to see more of Nora in the evenings than she was comfortable with. Not to mention that she had a feeling her dad and Nora wouldn't mind having a few evenings together without worrying about her. "The only problem I see is that until your part-time help gets well, you're here by yourself too much. Let me come in every day—at least through the rush time—and help you out."

"Rae, you are here to visit with your dad, and I have you working three nights as it is. You won't be able to spend that much time—"

"In case you haven't noticed—and granted, busy as you are,

you probably haven't—my dad is seeing someone," Rae teased. "I'm sure they won't mind. I'm staying through the New Year. Dad and I will have plenty of time together. I don't want to wear out my welcome, you know."

"I doubt you'd ever do that. But I can use the help, so I'll let you work as much as you want until Jen gets well—but only if you are sure."

"I'm sure." Rae was just relieved that she wouldn't have to spend every night trying to pretend that seeing her dad and Nora together didn't make her feel more alone than ever.

six

Rae did run to her dad's to change into clothes and shoes that were more comfortable. Taking a cue from what Dee usually wore, she put on jeans and a long-sleeved, lightweight top. She was glad she'd brought her walking shoes; they had to be more comfortable than the loafers she'd worn all day.

Before heading back to the diner, she called her dad's office to let him know she'd be working at the diner that night and not to worry about her for supper. His office manager assured Rae that he would get the message. The evening rush was just beginning when she returned to help Dee.

Rae knew that the amount of on-the-job training she received in the next few hours would go a long way toward preparing her for the next few weeks. It was a bit embarrassing when she got two tables' orders mixed up and sloshed coffee over the sides of a cup as she set it on the table. But the customers were very kind—especially after Dee told them Rae had taken pity on her and offered to help out until Nelda got back.

She half expected her dad and Nora to show up and was relieved when they didn't. They were probably enjoying the evening without her.

The lull after the supper rush was a welcome one, and Rae gladly took a break. She'd just asked Joe to make her a cheeseburger when she whirled around to find Luke walking toward the counter. He had on a jeans and a plaid western shirt that made his shoulders seem even broader. Her heart hammered in her chest at the sight of him, and she realized she had been waiting for him to come in all evening.

"Hi, Rae." Luke sat on the same stool he was on the day they met. "Is Dee going to work you all night?"

"No. I'm not," Dee answered, coming up behind him. "In fact, I'm sending her home after she eats. But I sure don't know what I would have done without her help today. I was about ready to throw in the towel and lock the door to this place."

"Yeah, right."

"I was. But Rae came to my rescue, and I'm extremely grateful."

Rae felt the heat of embarrassment flood her face while Dee talked about her as if she wasn't standing right there. "Please, you tried to help me find Dad the other night. I'm certainly not doing anything you wouldn't do for me."

"Well, still—"

"Luke," Rae interrupted Dee, "did you want something to eat?"

"Matter of fact, I do. How about some breakfast?"

"Breakfast?"

"Sure. I like it best at night." He rose up off the stool and called, "Joe!"

The cook appeared at the service window and handed Rae a plate containing her burger and fries. "Yeah, Luke. What you need?"

"How about making me one of those big fat omelets with ham and cheese and green chilies?"

"Okay," Joe said. "Hash browns on the side?"

Luke thought for a minute. "Yeah. . .make 'em really crispy, please."

"Will do."

Luke sat back down, and Dee brought him a cup of coffee and a large glass of orange juice.

Rae brought her plate to the counter and took a seat beside Luke. Her heart skipped several beats when he winked at her. He really was one handsome man.

"If you stay long enough, you'll be able to read my mind like Dee just did," he said, handing her the ketchup bottle Dee set on the counter.

"You think so?" Rae chuckled. She just hoped he couldn't read hers. Butterflies seemed to take flight in her stomach when her hand brushed his. How could she possibly be having this kind of reaction to any man after what she'd gone through the past few months? She couldn't—wouldn'—let herself be attracted to Luke.

Joe brought out Luke's meal along with the BLT Dee had evidently ordered and stood talking to them for a few minutes. Rae was glad she didn't have to carry the conversation, and she finished her cheeseburger as quickly as she could without choking on it.

She took her plate into the kitchen and came back out to find the last customers, all except for Luke, just leaving. Dee followed them to the door and flipped the sign in the window from Open to Closed.

Rae was immensely glad that Dee closed at nine o'clock Monday through Thursday nights. On Fridays and Saturdays, she stayed open until midnight.

"You can go on home, Rae. I'll finish up for tonight."

"What else needs to be done?" Rae was sure there was more to do than lock the door for the night.

"I just need to fill the sugar and sweetener containers and the salt and pepper shakers. Make sure the ketchup and mustard bottles are changed out, if need be. That kind of stuff."

"I can help. That way you'll get to go home earlier." Rae took the big box of sugar and sweetener packets from under the counter and began to fill the containers at the tables, while Dee filled salt and pepper shakers.

Luke was just finishing a second cup of coffee when they got through. He stood to pay Dee and glanced over at Rae. "I saw your car down the street. I'll walk you to it."

Downtown Sweet Springs seemed to close up early during the week, and it was dark and chilly outside. Rae took him up on the offer. "Thanks."

"I forgot to tell you; you can park out back of the diner. It's well lit back there. I bet you had a hard time finding a place to park when you came back from changing."

Rae pulled on her lightweight jacket as they walked to the door. "I only had to drive around the block a couple of times. I'll park in back next time."

"Okay. Thanks again, Rae. See ya, Luke." Dee closed and locked the door behind them.

Luke placed his hand at her back as they started down the street toward her car. Rae tried to ignore the way it made her feel special and protected—and the way her heart thudded with each step she took.

"What did Michael think about you working tonight?" he asked.

"I haven't talked to him. I left a note when I went home to change, but I'm sure he is fine with it. He's not used to having me underfoot. I imagine he and your aunt had a nice evening without me."

They arrived at her car and when she pulled her keys out of her pocket, Luke took them from her. After unlocking her car, he opened the door and watched as she slid in behind the steering wheel. When Rae took the keys back, static electricity shot up her arm, and she dropped the keys on the ground.

"Whoa! That was some shock." Luke chuckled and bent to pick them up.

Rae caught her breath as he leaned into the car and put the key in the ignition for her. His gaze met hers and lingered a moment before he backed out of the car.

"It really is nice of you to help Dee out." Luke looked down at her. "Jake told me Sara wants to have you over for supper. Can I tell them what night you might be free?"

"We don't have a hard-and-fast schedule for me to work. Dee is trying not to give me too many hours, but I'm planning on helping as much as I can. Early in the week would probably work best since the diner seems especially busy on Friday and Saturday nights."

"I'll tell Sara to call you." Luke smiled down at her. "You know your way to your dad's in the dark?"

Rae nodded. "I can find my way. Thanks."

A stiff breeze blew down the street and into the car. Rae shivered, and Luke moved to shut her car door. "Okay. I'll be seeing you."

"Night." Rae started her car. Only when she pulled out of her parking space and headed down the street did she breathe easy. Those warm brown eyes could sure take a girl's breath away.

∂⯌

Luke watched the taillights of Rae's car disappear around the corner before pulling the collar of his jacket up around his neck and jogging to his pickup. It was becoming cooler, just as the weather report had predicted.

He climbed into his truck and started it up, then rubbed his hands together, waiting for the engine to warm up before switching on the heater. He hadn't meant to come into town for supper tonight, but his curiosity had gotten the best of him, and he'd found himself driving by just to see if Rae's car was at Michael's. When he saw both cars gone, he decided to check the diner.

He could tell from her comment that she still wasn't happy about her dad and his aunt seeing each other. At least she didn't seem to be holding it against him, although Luke sensed she was keeping her distance from him. And he'd do well to do the same thing. Just because she was helping Dee out didn't mean she was going to stay in Sweet Springs forever. He had no business being this interested in her. None at all.

But how could I stifle that interest? he wondered as he rounded the curve to his brother's house. It was easy to say he wasn't going to let himself be attracted to Rae and quite another to keep his pulse from racing each time he saw her. She'd been adorable tonight, blushing as he and Dee talked about her. And when he'd put her key in the ignition for her, the vulnerable expression in her eyes had him wanting to protect her and kiss her all at the same time.

He really wasn't sure what to think of her, but the fact that she'd offered to help Dee out had changed his initial opinion of her. Luke had to admit that he'd been judging her without really knowing her. And he knew better.

He pulled into Jake's driveway and turned off the engine. Maybe Sara would have a cake or some kind of pie—she almost always did. He ran up the walk and knocked on the door. He'd learned not to ring the doorbell at this time of night. They might have just put Meggie down for the night and wouldn't be too happy if he woke her.

Sara opened the door and let him in. "I told Jake that it was you. You have a knack for knowing when I make my chocolate fudge cake. I just iced it."

Luke sniffed deeply and appreciatively. "Oh, I do love that cake."

He followed his sister-in-law into the kitchen where Jake was pouring three cups of coffee. Sara cut a third piece of cake and put it on a dessert plate.

"My Meggie asleep?"

"We just put her to bed. Not as easy to do now that she's walking *and* climbing."

Luke chuckled. Last time he was over, Meggie had managed to climb out of her bed to come see him. "I should have come a little earlier."

Sitting down at the table, Luke didn't waste any time in forking into his piece of cake. He loved the moist cake with the thick chocolate icing. It was one of his favorites. "Mmm. And to think I nearly went home without stopping by."

"What are you in town this time of night for anyway?" Jake asked.

Luke shrugged and took another bite.

"Jake told me that Rae offered to help Dee out. Was she still working tonight?" Sara asked.

"Yes, she was." Luke took a drink of coffee.

"And you ate supper at the diner, right?" Luke didn't immediately answer, and Jake pressed, "Didn't you?"

"It was late when I got through working, and I was hungry."

"I asked you to come over here."

"It's not nice to just show up after you've declined an invitation, Brother."

Sara chuckled and shook her head. "Luke Breland. You know you don't have to have an invitation to eat with us."

"I know. I did tell Rae you wanted to have her over."

"And?"

"She suggested early in the week. She thought Dee might need her more later in the week. I told her you'd call."

"Good. I will call and set something up with her. And I'll let you know when, okay?"

Luke tried to pretend he didn't understand what Sara was talking about. "Why?"

"Because I told her you'd use that rain check for when we had Rae over, just like you told me." Jake punched his brother's shoulder.

"Maybe that's not a good idea."

"Why not?"

"I don't have any business getting interested in her."

"She's cute. And she seems real sweet," Sara commented.

Luke sighed deeply. "And she's going back to Albuquerque after the holidays."

Jake got up to refill their coffee cups. "A lot can happen in a couple of months, little brother."

"Yeah, right." Luke took another bite of cake. His heart could be broken in that time frame.

After his second piece of cake, Sara wrapped up a third piece for him to take home. He left feeling a little forlorn. He loved being at Jake and Sara's, but at the same time, being around them always made him long for a family of his own.

He couldn't be anything but happy for them, though. It'd taken them years to finally get together. Jake and Sara had started out as high school sweethearts, but a serious misunderstanding broke them up, and Jake had married while away at college; then Sara had ended up marrying Nora's son, Wade. Several years ago, Wade had died in a car wreck, and a few months later Jake's wife died giving birth to Meggie. When Jake moved back to Sweet Springs this past spring, he and Sara had fallen in love all over again and were married on the Fourth of July.

They had something special, that was for sure. And he wanted the same thing. But he'd about given up on ever finding that special someone—in spite of the attraction he felt for Rae Wellington now. He couldn't afford to let himself begin to care about her. They were too different. She was definitely a city girl. And he was all country.

❧

Rae drove home trying to put thoughts of Luke out of her mind. She was aware it was static electricity that had shocked them both, but it was his lingering gaze in the car that had her heart skittering in her chest. For a moment, she'd thought he was going to kiss her. And she'd wanted him to.

He was fast making thoughts of Paul disappear, and while she wanted to quit thinking about her ex-fiancé, she wasn't quite ready to be thinking so much about another man. Especially one so different from her.

While Luke seemed totally comfortable with who he was,

she had a hard time picturing him being at ease around her friends in Albuquerque. But then she hadn't felt at ease around any of them since her and Paul's breakup. In fact, she hardly ever saw most of them now—funny how they'd kind of dropped her when she wasn't part of a couple anymore.

She'd found out pretty quickly how strong her friendships were, and it had become glaringly apparent they'd been much weaker than she'd thought. It all contributed to her decision to take a leave of absence.

She pulled into her dad's drive to find his car gone and entered the empty house to find a note from him. *Honey, I went to Nora's for supper. Will be home around ten. Hope Dee didn't work you too hard.*

Rae wasn't surprised—it was what she expected and the main reason she'd been glad to help Dee long-term. The way she saw it, Dee was helping her just as much as she was helping her new friend. She didn't want to be alone in Albuquerque, but she didn't want to have to endure Nora's company every night either.

Rae knew she wasn't being quite fair. Her dad had loved her mother with all of his heart, and he had every right to make a new life for himself. Just because she didn't have anyone to love didn't mean he shouldn't. Still, she couldn't make herself like Nora, but she had to try to for her dad's sake.

Trying to put it all out of her mind, she hurried to take a quick shower before her dad got home. Maybe she'd make him some hot chocolate tonight.

She wasn't fast enough, however. Dad had the chocolate mixture simmering when she entered the kitchen. He met her with a hug and a smile.

"I bet you're tired."

"A little." Rae took a seat at the kitchen island. She hadn't realized just how worn-out she was until she'd stood in the shower and let the warm water wash over her.

"You did eat, didn't you?"

"Of course, I did. A free meal is one of the perks of my new job. Did you and Nora have a nice time?"

He poured the hot chocolate into two mugs and handed her one. "We did. Missed you, though. You aren't going to be working all the time, are you?"

"No, of course not. But you don't need me underfoot every night."

"Honey, I love having you here. And Nora knows it. . .she's glad you're here too."

Oh, I just bet she is. Rae felt bad for the thought. She wasn't being fair to Nora, but she couldn't seem to help it. She had to try harder to accept the woman. "Thanks. But Dee needs the help right now, and I need something to do when you are at work. Besides, since I'm staying awhile, we'll have plenty of time to visit."

"All right. As long as you're okay with it. Will you mind having Thanksgiving dinner at Ellie's?"

Rae grinned. She'd been afraid they were going to have to eat at Nora's—or have her here. "That would be wonderful! I'll have to ask her what I can bring."

"I'm sure it will be a lot of fun. Nora's whole family will be there."

"Great!" Rae found she really was excited about going to Gram's for Thanksgiving. She'd get to visit more with her. And Sara and Jake and Meggie. *And. . .Luke.* Her heart skittered at the thought of him, and Rae sighed. How was she going to stop it from doing that?

seven

By Wednesday evening, Rae *almost* felt like a professional waitress. She'd even earned a few tips in the last few days. She didn't know how Dee put in the hours she did, and she was very glad to have the evening off.

She felt more comfortable at midweek church services too. Many of the members frequented the diner, and she'd even waited on a few of them. The class was beginning an in-depth study about putting one's trust in God, and Rae realized she needed to do a lot more trusting in the Lord to guide her than she had in the past year.

After class, it was good to have a chance to talk to Luke's grandmother again.

"Hello, Rae, Dear. I hear you've been pretty busy helping Dee out this week."

"Yes, Ma'am, I have." She wondered if it was Luke or Nora who'd told Gram about her working at the diner.

"Well, I hope you'll be able to come by and see me sometime this week. But I'd really like you to come help us stuff teddy bears this weekend, if you can find the time. We're meeting here in the fellowship hall, this Saturday morning at ten-thirty. We'll have a bite to eat afterward too."

"Oh, I'll be sure to make time! Dad has told me how the little bears you all make truly help the children who are brought into the emergency room at the hospital! I may not be able to stay for lunch; I'll probably help Dee out during the lunch rush, but I'd love to come help stuff bears."

"Wonderful!"

"I couldn't help but overhear your conversation," Nora said

from behind Rae. "I'll be glad to bring Rae with me, Ellie."

Rae took a deep breath and turned to Nora with what she hoped was a smile. "Don't worry about me, Nora. I can get here on my own. I'll be helping Dee out at the diner and will probably just come from there and go back."

Gram bobbed her head. "Whatever will be best for you, Dear."

"But I don't mind—"

"Nora, Dear, that makes perfect sense," Gram insisted. "That way you can help me set up and clean up."

"All right, Ellie," Nora agreed. She smiled at Rae. "I'm just glad you are coming to help us. You'll get to meet a few of the young women your age too."

Relieved that she wouldn't have to come with Nora, Rae's answering smile didn't feel quite so tight this time. "I'm looking forward to it."

Nora was called away just then by a lady about her age, and Rae turned back to Ellie. "It's been good to see you again, Gram. I've been meaning to ask for your cake recipe."

The older woman patted her on the shoulder. "I'll be sure and get it to you. And, Rae, Dear. . .Nora means well, you know?"

Embarrassed that Gram seemed able to read her so well, Rae felt the color creep up her cheeks. "I'm sure she does. I guess I'm just having a hard time accepting that Dad cares about someone else besides Mom. And I—"

"That's perfectly normal, Dear. And I know it can take some getting used to. I'm sure you are trying."

Rae felt her blush deepen. She wasn't trying, not really. And she had a feeling Gram saw through her excuses. She bit her bottom lip and glanced up. "I—"

The older woman looked into her eyes and smiled. "I'll say a prayer that it gets easier for you, Rae. You try to get by to see me soon as you can, all right?"

"I will. And. . .thank you."

"It will be all right, Dear. Just hand it all over to the Lord."

"You ready to go, Ellie?" William Oliver asked as he walked up to them. He smiled at Rae. "Hello, Rae."

"Hello, Mr. Oliver. How are you tonight?"

"I'm just fine. But this lovely lady seems a little tired to me. I think it's about time I took her home."

"Yes, Dear, I'm ready to go. I am a little tired tonight." She chuckled. "I watched Meggie for a little while today, and, oh, I just wish I had half her energy!"

Will laughed. "Don't we all!"

"Good night, Dear." Gram patted Rae's shoulder. "I'll see you soon, I hope."

"Yes, Ma'am." Rae watched the older couple walk off just as Sara walked up to her.

"I so wish those two would get married," Sara said, her gaze on her dad and Gram.

"They seem to care for one another a lot."

"Oh, they do. The whole family has been hoping they'll set a date one of these days. They spend most of their free time together anyway, and both live in houses that are way too big for one person. Besides, anyone can see they're crazy about each other."

Rae watched as Will leaned down to hear something Gram was saying to him. He nodded and grinned at her. "They do make a cute couple."

"Yeah, they do. And Michael and Nora make a beautiful one." Sara motioned in the direction of the fellowship hall where they could see the two talking and laughing with each other.

They do make a beautiful couple, Rae admitted to herself. And her dad was happier than she'd seen him in a long time. *Still. . .*

"Rae, I've been meaning to call you. I'd like to have you over for dinner one night soon. Can you tell me what night would be good for you? I don't know how often you'll be working."

"How nice of you!" Rae was glad that Sara had interrupted her thoughts. "My schedule at Dee's is pretty flexible, but she says Monday through Wednesday are her slowest nights. . .Thursday isn't too bad, but I'd hate to leave her alone for the weekend."

"How about next Monday night, then? Would that work?"

"Oh, I'm sure it will." Everyone was being so nice to her, trying to make her feel welcome. And she really liked Sara and Jake.

"About six-thirty?" Sara asked.

"That's fine with me. I'm looking forward to it!"

Sara grinned. "Good! I guess I'd better go rescue Luke. It appears that Jake handed Meggie off to him."

Through the window at the back of the sanctuary, which was open to the fellowship hall, Rae could see Luke holding his niece. He seemed completely captivated by whatever she was saying to him. "He doesn't seem to mind watching her."

"Oh, he doesn't. I'm just afraid of what she might talk him into. He's a pushover for anything that child wants."

Sara knew her brother-in-law well, Rae decided as they watched him pull a sucker out of his pocket, unwrap it, and hand it to his niece.

"Uh-oh! I'd better go. I'll talk to you later." Sara hurried off toward Meggie and Luke.

Rae chuckled as she gathered her Bible and purse and started up the aisle. Her dad seemed to have disappeared, and she was pretty sure he'd walked Nora to her car. Deciding to go on to the car, she made her way to the front door where she was greeted by the minister, David Morgan, and his wife, Gina.

"Rae Wellington, it's so good to finally meet you! I tried to get to you on Sunday to welcome you, but you were gone before I could."

"Now, David, that sounds as though Rae ran out of here. You were just caught up greeting others," Gina said. "Sometimes he puts his foot in his mouth, and things come out wrong."

Rae chuckled. Gina was sweet. "That's all right. He preaches a good sermon, though."

Gina smiled up at her husband and nodded. "He does. And that's what he's here for, isn't it?"

"Why, thank you, ladies. I am sorry, Rae. I certainly didn't mean it to sound the way it might have. At any rate, we're very glad to meet you now. Michael says you are staying through New Year's Day."

"I am. I thought it was about time I saw where Dad had decided to live the rest of his life, and he's talked me into staying awhile."

"And what do you think of Sweet Springs? Do you like it?"

Rae chuckled and inclined her head. "Better than I thought I would, actually. But don't tell Dad. I want to enjoy giving him a hard time about moving away from me for a little longer."

Both David and Gina chuckled. "Just so long as you like it here. Any chance of getting you to move here?"

"Oh, no. Albuquerque is home. But Sweet Springs is—"

"A nice place to visit?" Luke asked.

Rae's heart jumped. She hadn't realized he'd walked up behind her. "I've visited worse."

David chuckled. "I would hope so!"

"Oh, now I'm sorry! I guess I don't know how to word things any better than you—" Rae clapped her hand over her mouth as David, Gina, and Luke all burst out laughing. "I am *sooo* sorry."

"Don't worry about it, Rae. It made me feel better somehow."

Gina punched David's shoulder and shook her head. "It's

all right, Rae. We know you didn't mean anything by that."

"Oh, I think she did," Luke teased.

Rae ignored him. "Thank you, Gina."

"Guess I'd better go." Luke started for the door. "See you all later. Got to go wash some of the sticky from Meggie's sucker out of my hair."

Rae fixed her gaze on him and giggled. Luke's hair was sticking up in a few places, but he didn't really seem to mind.

"That Meggie is something, isn't she?" Gina asked. "I nearly lost it one Sunday when I saw her sticking a sucker in Sara's hair. It was all I could do to keep from laughing out loud."

"She's a cutie. I'll have to watch for her on Sunday," Rae said.

"She's some competition for my sermons, that's for sure." David shook his head. "Half the congregation watches that child."

Luke laughed. "And to think she's *my* niece."

"Uh-huh." David laughed. "Picked up some of your ornery too."

"That's what makes her so much fun." Luke grinned and headed out the door. "See you later."

"Good night, Luke," Gina said and waved at him.

"Night," Rae added. *He sure is cute with his hair sticking up like that.*

She saw her dad stop and speak to him for a moment before making his way back inside. "Hi, Honey. I just saw Nora off. Are you ready to go home?"

Rae chuckled. "Yes. I think I am. I need to go pull my foot out of my mouth."

"Night, Rae," David said. "When you figure out how, you let me know, okay?"

"I will." Rae giggled.

"Good night, Rae. We'll have to get together sometime soon," Gina suggested.

Rae nodded. "I'd like that. Good night."

"What was that all about?" Dad asked on the way to the car.

"Oh, nothing; just some teasing is all."

He smiled. "I'm glad you're feeling more comfortable here, Honey."

So was she—except around Nora and Luke. Nora, because Rae admitted, deep down, she wasn't really giving the older woman a chance to become friends; but she was especially uncomfortable around Luke. He made her heartbeat flutter and her pulse shaky. She had to get over the attraction she felt for him. She wasn't going to put herself in a position to get hurt again. She just wasn't.

Dear Lord, please keep me from going through that again. Please. In Jesus' name, amen.

❧

Luke stopped in at the diner before going home. He always felt a little lonely going home right after church. Seemed like everyone he knew was the other half of a couple—even Gram had Will to take her home. Luke had no one to take home. He'd have liked to have asked to see Rae home, but after overhearing her conversation with Gina and David, he realized he'd be much better off spending as little time in Rae's company as possible. He was very attracted to her. . .and it wasn't going to do him a bit of good. She would be going back to Albuquerque as soon as the holidays were over; she'd made that clear. There was no sense leaving himself wide open to being hurt when she left.

"Why so quiet, Luke?" Dee asked as she set his cup of hot chocolate in front of him. "Did you lose your best friend?"

"I don't think so, have I?" He grinned at her. She *was* one of his best friends, aside from his brother and cousin. He'd gone to high school with Dee, and she understood him well. He probably read her better than she wanted him to also. And if she and his cousin, John, ever got their heads out of the sand, she'd be part of his family.

Dee sat down beside him with her own cup of cocoa. "No, not if you mean me. But you sure seem sad tonight."

Luke grunted. "You know, it kind of makes you wonder what's wrong with you when even your grandmother is seeing someone and you aren't. Maybe I'm just too picky."

"Maybe we both are." She blew on her steaming drink before taking a sip. "Or maybe we're just too stubborn. Neither of us wants to move anywhere else, and we can't seem to fall for anyone who wants to stay."

Luke laughed. "You know, if this were a movie or a book, we'd end up with each other."

Dee laughed and spewed out the drink she'd just taken. She began coughing, and Luke patted her on the back. "I'm sorry. Didn't mean to choke you. The thought of falling for me is that funny, huh?"

Dee was still chuckling as she got up to clean up the mess she'd made on the counter. "We know each other maybe too well?"

"No. We just aren't each other's type." Luke shrugged. "But I'm beginning to wonder if I'm *anyone's* type."

"I don't even want to find out if I *am* anyone's type anymore. I'm too busy and too tired to care. It sure has helped having Rae here. I think God must have sent her here just to help me out."

"Oh? And here I was hoping He'd sent her here just for me. See how wrong I get things?" Luke chuckled and shook his head.

Dee saw through his teasing, though. "You really like her, don't you?"

"Won't do me any good. She's one of those city girls who doesn't want to move here."

"You never know. She could change her mind."

Luke shook his head. "No. She's planning on going back

after the holidays. Just remind me of that every now and then, okay?"

"A lot can happen in six weeks, Luke."

A lot could happen in a week. A heart could beat faster and attraction could bloom. But that didn't mean a happy ending was always in store. If he'd learned anything in his thirty-four years, it was that. *But, Lord, I sure would like it if Rae decided she loved it here yes, Sir, I sure would.*

❧

"I'm kind of hungry. Want to stop at the diner and get a piece of pie and coffee?" Rae asked her dad.

"I'm always ready for pie and coffee, but aren't you kind of tired of the place?"

"No, not really." She thoroughly enjoyed the diner. It was so totally different from what she usually did that she was honestly having a good time. "Besides, it's not the same as being a customer. And if Dee is busy, I can get our order myself."

But Dee wasn't too busy to wait on them. It was only she and Luke at the counter, and a young couple at one of the booths.

"Well, hey there. Guess we all had the same idea, didn't we?" Luke asked.

Be still, my heart. Rae was almost getting accustomed to the way her heartbeat sped up each time she saw Luke—no matter how many times she told it not to. But he did look so endearing tonight, smiling at them. . .with his hair still all spiky in places. It appeared he'd tried to smooth it down, but it hadn't cooperated.

"I guess we did," Dad said. He sat down at the table closest to the counter. "Why don't you two join us over here?"

Rae quickly slid in beside her dad, while Luke unwrapped his legs from around the bar stool, grabbed his cup, and sauntered over. "Sure."

"Let me take your order." Dee pulled out her order pad.

"Then I'll join you."

"We just want some of that apple pie and coffee." Rae saw the young couple head toward the cash register. "But I can get it while you ring them up."

"Nah. You ring and I'll wait."

"Okay." Rae slipped out of the booth and went to ring them, and while Dee was dishing up their pie, she cleaned off the table the young people had left.

When she returned to the table, her pie and coffee were waiting for her. She slid into the booth and glanced up to see Luke studying her with his warm brown gaze. Feeling her face flush, she forced herself to look down at her plate and fork a bite of pie.

"Nora tells me the ranch is really flourishing under your management, Luke," Dad said. "She says you've set up a new computer bookkeeping system that has streamlined everything."

Luke grinned and nodded. "Those classes I took really helped. Uncle Ben seems happy with the changes. We're able to keep track of our livestock much better now. Not to mention our supplies and our cash flow."

Rae breathed a sigh of relief when Luke and her dad launched into a thirty-minute conversation about ranching. *Thank you, Dad.* It gave her time to get her bearings, get her heart rate back down to normal.

She and Dee were too tired to talk much. Rae asked about Nelda and found Dee hadn't heard any more from her. Dee finished her coffee and got to her feet. "You all can stay, long as you like, but I'm closing up."

"I'll help." Rae slid out of the booth.

"You don't have to do that."

"I know. But you'll get home earlier if I do."

"Thanks, Rae."

Dee went to count the cash drawer, and Rae got up to help with the closing. She filled the napkin dispensers and made sure the various containers were filled, then wiped down all the tables. During all of it, she enjoyed the murmur of her dad and Luke's conversation in the background, interspersed with their masculine laughter. It was obvious that they liked and respected one another.

By the time they were through getting everything ready for the next morning, Luke and Dad were on their feet and standing at the door.

"Guess, I'd better go on home, or Dee will lock up with me still here. See you all later." Luke headed out the door.

"We're leaving too." Her dad waited for Rae to get her jacket on.

"Brrr—it's cold out here," Luke said, pulling the collar up on his jacket as the cold night air hit him.

Rae and her dad waited until Dee locked up behind them before they headed for his car. But as she watched Luke get into his truck and drive off with a wave, she felt a tug at her heart and wondered why it was that he was the one driving off alone. . .yet she'd never felt quite so lonely in her life.

eight

The next few days, Rae took it upon herself to help Dee during the rush hours. Dad left early to make rounds at the hospital, and Rae got in the habit of making a quick breakfast for the two of them, then leaving the house about the same time he did.

She was beginning to put names to faces, and there were a few of Dee's customers who were fast becoming her favorites. One was old Mr. Babcock. The ninety-year-old man was definitely—and justifiably—set in his ways. He liked his bacon crisp and his eggs over easy, with hash browns and toast on the side. He ate slowly and watched everything that went on in the diner, making entries into a notebook every once in awhile. Dee explained that he was writing a book about life in a small town. He'd told Dee that her character's name would be Darla.

When he came to the register to pay for his breakfast Saturday morning, Rae figured she'd been accepted. He leaned over the counter and whispered, "Your name will be Marla. You and Darla will be sisters who run the local diner."

"Why, Mr. Babcock. I'm honored to have a place in your book."

He patted her hand. "You earned it by coming to Dee's aid."

Rae shook her head as she watched him shuffle out the door. He was a real sweetheart. She turned to Dee. "Guess what? You and I are sisters in Mr. Babcock's book!"

Dee chuckled. "I know. He told me. Said I'd have to share ownership of the diner."

They were still laughing when Luke and Jake entered with a man Rae had never seen. He was tall, like Luke and Jake, only his hair was lighter and his eyes were hazel. But it was Dee's sharp intake of breath that told Rae this man wasn't a stranger—at least not to her. It was curious how the usually unflappable Dee seemed to be suddenly fidgety.

She turned away quickly and gathered menus and water glasses, but Rae could see her hands slightly shaking. She peered over to where the three men had taken a seat and found that the man with them was watching Dee closely.

"Do you want me to wait on them?" Rae asked.

"No, I've got it, thanks. Besides, aren't you supposed to be at church to stuff bears pretty soon?"

"Oh, you're right!" Rae checked the clock over the jukebox. "Thanks for reminding me—I'd better get a move on. I'll be back to help with lunch."

"You don't have to do that—"

"I know, but I want to." She took off her apron and hung it on a hook just inside the kitchen, put on her jacket, and grabbed her purse. She'd stepped out front to ask Dee what time she should be back when Luke waved her over.

"Hey, Lady, where you going in such a hurry?"

"I'm on my way to church. Gram asked me to help stuff teddy bears."

"Whoa! You'd better be off, then. Gram will wonder where you are. But before you go, meet our cousin, John. This is Dr. Mike's daughter, Rae, John."

"Pleased to meet you, Rae," John said, rising from his chair.

Rae waved him to sit back down. "I'm glad to meet you too, John. I'm sorry I'm in such a rush—"

Luke shooed her away. "It's all right. We know how Gram feels about people being on time. You go on. You'll see plenty of John while he's here."

"Okay, I'll see y'all later."

ھ

Luke watched as Rae rushed out the door. Seemed like he only saw her in short spurts of time. It probably was better this way, though, because he was having a really hard time trying to get her out of his mind. Seeing more of her certainly wouldn't help that lost cause.

Dee brought water and menus to the table, and he switched his attention to watch how she and John reacted to each other.

"Well, what do we have here?" Dee asked with a smile. "It's good to see you, John."

"It's good to see you too, Dee. How's business?"

"A little too good sometimes." Dee sighed as two more patrons came in. "Do you know what you want?"

"We'll make it easy on you, Dee. Give us the daily specials," Jake said. "That okay with you two?"

"Fine with me." Luke handed his menu back to Dee. "And coffee, please."

"Same here, Dee." John gave her his menu.

She hurried off to get water for the couple that had come in.

"She works too hard," John said.

"Yes, she does," Jake agreed.

"I'm just glad Rae offered to help out. But I hope Jen comes back soon. Rae is here more than she's at Dr. Mike's." Luke was certain he'd given himself away. He just hoped Jake didn't pick up on it.

"Oh?" Jake raised an eyebrow at him, and Luke had no one to blame but himself for the question his brother asked next. "And how would you know that?"

"I just know these things, that's all." Luke grinned. He wasn't about to tell them how many times he'd called the Wellington house only to get the answering machine.

"She seems nice," John said.

"She is. Just ask Dee." Jake motioned to his brother. "Or Luke."

"Aha." John chuckled and settled his gaze on Luke. "Two and two are beginning to add up here. Is she moving to Sweet Springs?"

Luke sighed. "No. She lives in Albuquerque and is just here until after the holidays."

"That's awhile. What does she do? Go from town to town rescuing the overworked?" John teased.

"She took a leave of absence from teaching high school," Luke said, realizing that he still didn't know why. And he didn't know how to ask without sounding really nosy. "That's all I know."

"Nora told Sara that Rae had a broken engagement several months back," Jake said and held up his hand as if he understood Luke was full of questions. "And that's all *I* know."

Well, that was more than he'd known before. A broken engagement. That *was* news and it explained a lot. He almost slapped his brother on the back to thank him for the information.

"How do she and Aunt Nora get along?" John asked.

"I think they walk softly around each other," Jake answered. "I'm pretty sure Nora would like to get to know her better, but—"

"Aunt Nora and Rae are both keeping so busy it isn't easy for them to get to know each other," Luke said.

Jake chuckled and shook his head. "No, it's not." He took a sip of tea before continuing. "And it's too bad. Aunt Nora has a big heart once you get to know her really well."

❧

Rae felt a little nervous as she entered the fellowship hall, but she was quickly put at ease by the ladies there. Gram welcomed her with a kiss on the cheek and patted the seat beside her. Nora smiled from across the table and began to introduce her to everyone.

She'd met Gina already, and then there were about ten other ladies she recognized either from seeing them at church or the diner.

Gram explained that several of the women embroidered the faces on the bears, and several others sewed them up, making sure to add a label that told the recipient's family that they'd been *Made with Love.* Then once a month everyone got together, stuffed them, and sewed up the bottom. Sara would deliver them to the hospital for the church.

Hopefully, the bear would give comfort to any child brought to the hospital. The label also gave the church's name, phone number, and address—just in case the parent was searching for a church home or needed comfort from the minister or one of the elders. They'd had several new members begin attending for that very reason.

Rae watched the teddy bear she was working on take shape as she stuffed it. Others who were more practiced at it already had several finished. The bears were adorable.

"Dad told me how well they're received. It's got to be a good feeling knowing that you've helped a child be a little less frightened about being in the hospital."

"It is," Gram said. "We didn't know how well they would go over when we first started earlier in the year. But we've already doubled our original output. We furnish them for the local fire and police stations. Ambulances too—just in case there's a child around that needs comforting."

Rae enjoyed the snippets of conversation around the table, letting her know these women loved each other. Sara showed up after dropping Meggie off at the church nursery where several of the teens were watching the younger children. She took a seat beside Rae.

"Hi! I'm glad you could make it, Rae."

"So am I." Rae worked a piece of stuffing down into one of the little bear's legs.

"How do you like working at the diner?" Nora asked from across the table.

"I like it a lot. It's quite a change from teaching, though."

"That's right." Gram glanced up from sewing. "It is high school you teach, right?"

"Ninth grade."

"Oh, wow." Sara shook her head. "I don't think I could handle that grade. I want to teach grade school when the children get—"

"The *children?*" Nora laid down the bear she'd been working on and peered across the table. "Sara, does this mean. . . ? Are you expecting?"

Everyone at the table stopped talking as if waiting for Sara's answer.

She blushed and smiled. "I am."

Nora jumped up and ran around to hug her. "Oh, how wonderful! I'm going to be a grandmother again!"

Sara patted Nora's back. "Yes, you are."

Rae was surprised to see tears in Nora's eyes. She seemed genuinely happy. Gram was wiping her eyes, as were many others. Rae must have looked confused, because Sara glanced at her and chuckled as she wiped away her own tears.

"Rae, you have to forgive us. I'm sure you don't know the whole story. I lost a baby when Wade and I were in the wreck that took his life." She glanced around the table, then back at Rae. "Without my family—Nora, Gram, and all the others—and this church family, I might not be here now to share my good news."

"Oh, Sara. . ." Rae swallowed around the lump in her throat at the thought of all Sara must have gone through.

"How is Jake doing?" Gram asked. "Walking on air?"

Sara sighed. "He's thrilled, of course. And a little nervous. Watches me like a hawk and treats me as if I'm made of eggshells."

"That's to be expected, you know." Nora had taken her seat again.

Sara smiled at Rae's unspoken question and explained. "Jake's first wife died giving birth to Meggie. He's a little apprehensive too."

"I can understand that." These new friends of hers had been through a lot of heartache before they found happiness. She would pray for all to go well with Sara's pregnancy.

"Well, he'll take wonderful care of you; I know that." Nora seemed to want to assure everyone. "How do you think my Meggie is going to react to a sibling?"

Everyone at the table chuckled.

"Well, I guess we'll see in about seven months. But it's bound to be real interesting, isn't it?"

Even Rae could laugh at that.

Once all the bears were stuffed, Gram, Nora, and several others began to set up the luncheon she'd mentioned, and Rae looked at the clock. "Oh, look at the time! I guess I'd better get back to the diner and help Dee."

"Are you sure you can't stay?"

"I'd better not, Gram."

"I wish you could stay and have a bite to eat with us," Nora added. "But it's so nice that you've offered to help Dee."

Now that Rae felt so welcome and at home, she almost wished she could stay. But it was Saturday, and the diner was bound to be busy. "I wish I could too. But I told Dee I'd be there. Thank you all for making me feel so welcome. Will you be stuffing bears again next month?"

"Oh, yes, we will."

"Maybe I can plan to stay for lunch, then." Rae put on her jacket and gave Gram a hug. Nora patted her on the back, and Sara walked her to the door.

"I'm really looking forward to Monday night," Sara said.

"So am I. Is there anything I can bring?"

"No. Just yourself. We'll see you tomorrow at church, okay?"

"Sure will." Rae waved to the other women. "See you all tomorrow!"

When she returned to the diner, Dee was swamped with customers, so Rae hurried to the back and put on her apron. It was midafternoon before they had a chance to do much more than smile at each other in passing.

"Whew! I'm glad you came back," Dee said as they took a quick coffee break about three o'clock. "But I have good news. Jen called, and she'll be back Monday evening. After she gets back, I think I can handle it with you helping just a few days a week."

"Oh, I know that's a relief for you, Dee. And I'm glad she's feeling better. Just know that I'm here and willing to help if you need me."

"I appreciate that more than I can tell you, Rae. I feel like we've become good friends in a short amount of time."

"Thanks, Dee. I feel the same way," Rae replied truthfully. It was a good feeling.

"Did you have a good time at church?"

"I did." Rae nodded. "Everyone made me feel so welcome. And the bears are so cute."

"That's good. I'm glad you went." Dee took a sip of coffee.

"Tell me again. . . . Who was that man with Luke and Jake this morning?"

"That's John, their cousin. He's Jake's law partner, but he's trying to decide whether to run for United States senator or not. I was so busy while they were here, I didn't have a chance to ask if he's made up his mind yet." She rubbed a finger around the rim of her cup and gazed out the window. "He'll make a good one."

There was a wistful sound in her voice, or so it seemed to Rae. She suspected Dee had mixed feelings about John running for office.

"Is he back for awhile?"

"I don't know. Probably. He's been testing the waters, so to speak. Lining up support and everything. I imagine he's close to making up his mind, but he'll probably be here until after the holidays." Dee gave the diner a once-over. "Which reminds me—I've got to decide how I'm going to decorate for Christ-mas. The downtown businesses try to outdo each other every year."

"Sounds like fun. If you need me to help, just let me know."

"Thanks! Once Jen gets back, and I don't need you to help here so much, maybe I can have you shop for decorations. I don't have much time. . ."

Rae was struck by just how little free time Dee seemed to have. "Dee, when Nelda is here and Jen is well, do you ever take any time off?"

"Oh, an afternoon here and there. Once in a while I take Wednesday night off."

"You need more help. You are going to wear yourself out. Your business seems to be thriving. . . . It can't be a matter of not having enough money to hire more help."

Dee shook her head. "No, I can afford it. I've been doing it this way so long—but lately I have felt like I was missing out. . .like there ought to be more to my life than just run-ning the diner."

"Is there anyone you're interested in dating?"

Dee got a faraway expression in her eyes and shook her head no, but the color creeping up her cheeks made Rae wonder.

"I just feel like life is passing me by sometimes." Dee got up to wipe a table. "Maybe I will hire someone else."

"Well, I'm here for awhile." Rae took their cups to the back and cleaned off the counter. "But I think you ought to have more help."

Dee chuckled. "I'll mull it over. Thanks."

❧

By the time Rae drove home that night, she was very glad the next day was Sunday. And she had to admit to herself that she was glad Dee's part-time help was coming back. She wanted to continue to help Dee, but she would also like time to spend with Sara and Gram and get to know their family better.

As for Nora. . .Rae still didn't much like her, but she'd certainly seen a different side of her today. She cared a lot about Sara; that'd been obvious. And she was very excited about the new baby. But much as she liked Nora's family, she just couldn't make herself like the older woman. She just seemed so. . .so. . .stiff most of the time. Or maybe it seemed she was trying too hard to be nice, and Rae had a feeling it was just for her dad's benefit. Still, Nora wasn't going anywhere. Rae was going to have to get used to her, like it or not.

Dad had called the diner earlier to let her know he was taking Nora to a Chinese restaurant for dinner and to see if she might be able to join them, so she was surprised to find that he was already home when she got there.

"Dad! I didn't expect you to be here," she said, entering the kitchen from the garage.

"Hi, Honey!" He called from the great room where he was watching the news. He came through to the kitchen and hugged her. "It's good to have you home! Nora knows we haven't spent a lot of time together since you've been here, and she suggested that it might be nice if I was here to make you a cup of hot chocolate when you got home."

Rae didn't much care whose idea it was. It was just good to have her dad there. "That was nice of her. And I'd love some, thanks."

"Want to go take a shower or bath first? I can have it ready when you get out."

"Oh, Dad, thank you! I will enjoy that chocolate a whole lot more after a shower."

"Go to it then."

Rae hurried down the hall. "Won't take me long."

And it didn't. The sweet scent greeted her as she walked back into the kitchen. "Mmm, that smells yummy, Dad."

He poured the mixture into two mugs. "It'll relax you for a good night's sleep. Want some marshmallows?"

At her nod, he plunked a handful of the miniature kind into her cup and added another handful to his before motioning her into the great room. Rae settled into a corner of the couch and gazed into the fire. She expelled a deep breath and took a sip from her cup.

"Honey, I'm afraid you are working too hard. I wanted you to have some time to relax and enjoy yourself while you are here."

"Don't worry, Dad. Dee's part-time help is coming back on Monday, and she may even hire another person. I won't have to work as much next week."

"Oh, good. I know Nora would like to take you to lunch or shopping sometime while you're here."

Rae chose not to comment on that little nugget of news. "I'm going to Sara and Jake's for dinner Monday night; did I tell you?"

"Yes, you mentioned it. You'll enjoy yourself. Sara is a great cook, and they are a nice couple. Is Luke going to be there?"

Rae's heart somersaulted at mention of the man she'd been trying so hard *not* to think about. So much for believing she had her attraction for Luke under control. "I don't know."

"Oh, I just wondered. Did he ever get in touch with you this evening?"

"No." Rae shook her head. "Was he supposed to?"

"Beats me. My caller ID just showed several calls from his house, but he didn't leave a message."

nine

Rae was still wondering what Luke had called about when she saw him sitting two pews in front of her at church. Maybe he'd let her know after church.

True to everything she'd heard, Meggie was an attention getter. She was up on the same pew as Luke and the rest of his family, and she was making faces at Luke. Rae could tell from the muffled sounds around her that she wasn't the only one fighting laughter.

It was only when Sara got up and took her stepdaughter to the nursery that Rae could concentrate on the sermon David was preaching. It was one she very much needed to hear—about growing closer to the Lord through prayer. Her prayer life had suffered recently, and she admitted it. It was spasmodic at best, and she knew she needed to pray more often. . .talk to the Lord they way she used to.

When the service was over, Rae was propelled out the door before she could talk to hardly anyone. Her dad and Nora wanted to take her to the Mexican restaurant they liked so well, and they were afraid they'd have to wait in line if they didn't hurry.

❧

"Why, Luke. . .check you out. Showing up for Gram's Sunday night supper two weeks in a row!" Jake teased as Luke walked up the steps to join him on the front porch of their grandmother's home.

"So?" Luke was aware that he sounded defensive. He hadn't been coming to the Sunday night suppers on a regular basis—or any of the family gatherings as often in the last several months. But he wasn't about to tell his brother that it'd been getting too hard to be the only single guy there. When John was in town, it wasn't so bad. Both bachelors, they were each other's support network. But while he'd been gone, Luke found it was easier to go home and watch a little television, take in a movie—anything besides watching his whole family carry on their romances right before his eyes.

Jake seemed to sense that Luke was in no mood to be teased and slapped his brother on the back. "So, nothing. It's just good to have you around."

"Thanks. I figured John could use some support. I know how it feels to be the odd man out around here." He could have kicked himself for giving away his feelings as he saw an ornery glint in his brother's eyes.

"Support for John, huh? I thought maybe it had something to do with the fact that Rae Wellington is in the kitchen helping Gram out."

Luke shook his head and tried to hide the fact that the possibility of seeing Rae did have a whole lot to do with his being there. And Dee's comment about a lot that could happen in six weeks kept coming back to him. Was it possible that Rae could learn to care about him and Sweet Springs? Was he willing to take a chance that the outcome would be one to his liking if he tried to get her to care?

Once inside the house, he tried not to make it obvious that he was headed to the kitchen, so he stopped to talk to several people along the way. He met up with John in the dining room and on the pretext of checking in with their grandmother, they both entered the kitchen. And there Rae was, flushed and smiling at something Gram was saying to her as Rae sliced several of the pies on the worktable.

"Luke—John, you showed up just in time," Gram said. "How about helping Rae get these desserts out to the dining room table?"

"I'd be glad to. John, you met Rae at the diner, right?" Luke asked, taking the two pie pans she handed him. Gram handed John a cake plate to take out.

"Briefly," John replied. "Sara introduced us again when I got here, but I haven't had a chance to thank her for helping Dee out while she's so shorthanded. She's a good friend of ours, and she works way too hard."

"Yes, she does. I've enjoyed helping out," Rae said.

"And now Gram has put you to work too." Luke grinned.

"I put everyone in my kitchen to work." Gram chuckled. "If you don't want to help, don't come in."

"But Rae didn't know that," Luke teased, winking at Rae.

Her color seemed to deepen as she glanced at him and shook her head. "Truth is, I had to just stand here, begging, until she gave me something to do."

Rae picked up two more pies and led the way to the dining room.

"I called last night to see if you might want to take in a movie this afternoon, but no one was at home." Luke set his pies on the table.

"I helped at the diner, and Dad and Nora went to dinner. Dad thought you might be trying to get in touch with me."

Luke's stomach did a nosedive. Michael evidently had caller ID too. Why had he not thought of that? He said a quick, silent prayer that Rae's dad hadn't told her how many times he'd called.

"Maybe you can take in a movie with us one night this week." He nudged his cousin.

If John was surprised at the invitation, he didn't say anything. "Sure would be nice to have some female company, Rae."

"Maybe I can," Rae said. "I don't think Dee is going to need me quite as much this next week. Her part-time help is supposed to be back. I am going to dinner at Sara and Jake's tomorrow night, and I'm looking forward to that."

"I'm sure they are too." Luke made a mental note to find his brother and ask why he hadn't mentioned this little detail when he was doing all his teasing about Rae. And he'd better be invited.

"So am I," John said. "Sara invited me too."

"And yes, Luke, you are invited. I wouldn't dare ask John and not you," Sara declared, walking up with Meggie. "I left a message on your answering machine because I didn't know if you would be here tonight or not."

"Well, it's a good thing you did. I was about to get jealous if John was invited and I wasn't!" He tweaked Meggie under her chin, and she immediately reached out to him.

"Unc' Luke, you gots a sucker?"

Luke took her in his arms and pointed to his shirt pocket. "No sucker tonight, Baby. Mommy said no more. But check in here and see what you can find."

Meggie reached in and pulled out a small, colorful packet. "Gummies! Tankie, Unc' Luke. I love gummies."

She handed the packet to him to open for her and kissed him on the cheek. At least Meggie loved him. "Look, Meggie, this is Mr. Mike's daughter, Rae. Have you met her?"

Meggie shook her head and smiled shyly at Rae. "Her's pretty."

"Yes, she sure is," Luke agreed.

Rae blushed and chuckled. "Thank you, Meggie. You are very pretty yourself."

Meggie bobbed her head up and down. "Tankie. You gots any suckers?"

Luke liked the way Rae rubbed Meggie's cheek and smiled. She shook her head. "I'm sorry, Sweetie, I don't."

"'S okay. I got gummies. Unc' Luke give me." She stuffed several in her mouth just before giving Luke a great big kiss on his cheek. A moment later she rubbed his head with a handful of gummies.

"Well, Miss Meggie, I can see I'm going to have to make a visit to the candy store," John said. "Uncle Luke has apparently been making the most of my absence."

"Can'y store?" Meggie asked.

"Yeah. Maybe I'll bring you something tomorrow night."

Meggie clapped her hands on Luke's head, smashing a gummy into it, and he laughed. "Might want to rethink that, John. Senatorial candidates aren't real appealing with sticky hair."

He handed Meggie back to Sara and asked, "Rae, will you help me get this gummy out of my hair?"

Rae laughed, seeming to find it all very funny as she followed him into the kitchen.

"That niece of yours is something." Rae was still chuckling as she pulled at the candy in his hair.

"Ouch!"

"I'm sorry. Let me get a damp paper towel and see if I can get some of the sticky off without pulling out too much of your hair."

Luke's heart thudded against his ribs as Rae gently rubbed his hair with the wet towel. The better he got to know this woman, the more he liked her. . .and the more he wanted to know about her.

"There, I think I got it all."

"Thank you." His pulse began to race as he gazed into her blue eyes and saw them sparkle with merriment.

A giggle escaped, bringing his gaze to her lips. "Meggie does a good job with those sticky hands of hers."

Luke couldn't tear his gaze away. He wanted to kiss her. "Yes, she does. I may have to find some kind of candy that's not sticky."

"I don't think that's possible," Rae said, sounding a little breathless.

Luke inclined his head closer. "With Meggie. . .probably. . .not."

The kitchen door suddenly swung open, and Rae quickly spun toward the sink.

Luke turned around to see who'd entered the kitchen and glared at his brother.

Jake looked from Luke to Rae, who had her back to him. He shrugged. "I was trying to find Sara."

"She's *not* here," Luke informed him.

"So I see." Jake backed out of the kitchen, mouthing a silent "sorry."

Luke rubbed the back of his neck, trying to figure out what to say next to Rae. He was embarrassed and was sure she was too. Had Jake not interrupted them, he would have kissed her. Now, he didn't know whether to be thankful or furious with his brother.

He turned to the woman he was beginning to care way too much for and reached out to touch her shoulder. He quickly lowered his hand as the door swung open once again.

"Oh, there you two are," Gram said. "I've worked you enough tonight, Rae. Come on out and enjoy yourself."

Somehow, Rae managed to move from the sink and get out the door without ever meeting his gaze, and Luke leaned against the counter and let out an exasperated sigh. He shook his head and rubbed his hand over his mouth. Pushing himself away from the cabinet, he headed for the dining room. He wanted to talk to Rae to see if he'd totally botched everything by nearly kissing her, and he hunted all over for her. But for the rest of the evening, she seemed to stay one step ahead of him.

❧

Rae offered to stay and help clean up, but Gram wouldn't let her. Nora insisted that Rae and her father go on home, saying she'd stay and help since Rae seemed tired.

She was tired. . .emotionally tired. She'd spent the better part of the night trying to avoid running into Luke when what she wanted most was to do just that. What must he think of her? When he'd looked at her there in the kitchen, she thought he might kiss her, like that night in her car. And she'd wanted him to. . .even more than she had then. More than she should. And she was afraid he could tell. He'd leaned toward her. . .his lips had been only inches from hers. And then Jake had come into the kitchen right before she'd melted into Luke's arms. She should probably be grateful that he'd interrupted them. . .but she couldn't quite manage to feel that way.

Yes, she was very attracted to Luke. She couldn't deny it. She really liked being around him, and she loved the way he responded to Meggie. Oh, how she wanted to get to know him better. What was she thinking? She was just getting over one broken relationship; the last thing she needed was to lose her heart to someone else. She was just going to *have* to distance herself from Luke.

Which was going to be much easier said than done, she realized, remembering that he'd be at Sara and Jake's for dinner the next night.

"You're awfully quiet over there," her dad commented as he drove her home. "You're not coming down with anything, are you?"

"No. I'm fine, Dad." And she was going to be. She wasn't going to lose her heart to Luke. She just wasn't.

Rae kept telling herself that all the next day while helping Dee out on the day shift. She was relieved that Luke didn't come in during the day, although Jake and John came in for lunch. Dee waited on them, and as Rae watched the give-and-take between her and John, she decided that there must be something going on between the two.

She dressed with care that evening as she got ready for dinner at Jake and Sara's. She put on a long black skirt and a red and black sweater. Needing all the confidence she could muster, she'd picked one of her favorite outfits. She pulled on her black boots, grabbed her leather jacket, and hurried down the hall.

It smelled wonderful in the kitchen. Her dad was cooking for Nora tonight, and he was making his special: taco soup. "Hmm, I almost wish I hadn't accepted Sara's invitation. It smells delicious, Dad. Want me to set the table before I go?"

"No, Honey. I'm fine. Nora will be here soon, and she'll do it."

"Okay." Rae pulled on her jacket. She kissed her father on the cheek and had started out to the garage when the doorbell rang. She glanced back at her dad and saw that he was in the middle of draining the potatoes. "That's probably Nora. I'll let her in."

She hurried through to the entryway and opened the door. Nora stood there with a cake in her hands and Luke peering over her shoulder.

"Surprise!" Nora hurried inside. "My car wouldn't start for some reason, and I asked Luke to give me a ride into town since he was coming in anyway."

"And since my truck is warm already, Aunt Nora suggested that you might want to ride with me. I can pick her up on the way back," Luke explained just as Michael walked up.

"That's a great idea, isn't it, Honey?" he asked, glancing at Rae.

So much for keeping my distance, Rae thought as she willed her heartbeat to slow down. "Great. Thank you."

"You're welcome. You ready?"

"I was just on my way to the car."

"Well, let's go, then."

Rae kissed her dad on the cheek once again. "See you two later."

"Have fun. Kiss Meggie for me," Nora added as Luke and Rae headed down the walk.

Luke opened the passenger door for her, and Rae got into his truck, glad for its warmth. She'd have been halfway across town before her car warmed up. She buckled up as Luke went around and got in on his side.

"It's getting colder. I wouldn't be surprised to see some snow by tomorrow," he said. "That'll put the downtown association into the mood to start thinking Christmas."

Relieved that he was keeping the conversation away from what nearly happened the night before, Rae relaxed. "When do they start decorating?"

"Most start the day after Thanksgiving, but some start earlier."

"Dee mentioned that she might want me to help her. I have to admit this cool weather helps. It's beginning to feel like Christmas, even though Thanksgiving isn't here yet."

It didn't take long to get to Jake and Sara's, as they lived downtown not far from Gram's. It was a new home but was built to look as though it'd been around since the turn of the century. The bay windows and large, wraparound porch made Rae feel as if she'd stepped back in time. Once inside the house, Rae was surprised to see that it was furnished in an eclectic mixture. The living room was done in antiques; the family room, comfortable traditional. The kitchen was thoroughly modern but made to appear old—and it worked beautifully. Wooden floors and cabinets warmed up the space around tiled countertops and gleaming fixtures.

"Oh, this is lovely, Sara."

"Thank you. It's actually a floor plan that Jake and I picked out when we were young and in high school. He kept it in mind for years, and now we have our dream home."

She checked the oven and pulled out an enchilada casserole that smelled wonderful.

"Is there anything I can do to help?"

"No." Sara shook her head. "We're eating here in the breakfast area, just because it's cozy and Meggie can play while we eat. I fed her earlier, and Jake is getting her out of the tub."

The doorbell rang and Luke went to answer it.

"That's probably John." Sara was right. Luke came back into the kitchen with John about the same time Jake came down the back staircase holding a clean and sweet-smelling Meggie. John gave her a kiss on the cheek, then tickled her. She giggled and almost jumped into his arms.

"I guess it's your night, John." Sara turned to Rae and explained. "Meggie doles out her attention in a very fair way. Last night it was Luke; tonight it's John. Next time, it will probably be you."

"How sweet."

"Well, it is once you figure it out—'cause when it's not your turn, it's not your turn. But when it is, she gives you her undivided attention." Luke proved his point by trying to get Meggie to come to him. She burrowed her head into John's shoulder, making Sara laugh and shake her head.

She set the casserole on the table, along with a salad and chips. "Come on, everyone. John, just sit Meggie in her chair by you. I'll give her some chips, but she'll want down to play in a few minutes."

Once seated, they all held hands as Jake prayed, thanking the Lord for their food and many blessings.

"We figured we'd better enjoy your company as long as we can, John," Jake said, dishing up a plate for his cousin. "After you become a senator, your visits will fly by and probably won't occur very often."

John nodded. "I know. But I'll be here as often as I can; you know that. I get my strength from the Lord and this family."

"Don't we all?" Jake handed a plate to Rae.

"Especially Gram," Sara added.

"You know, she told me she'd even campaign for me," John informed them.

"This whole family will be out there." Luke took the plate Jake handed him.

"Even you, Luke?"

"Well, of course. As much as I can. I can at least do some campaigning around here. I figure Uncle Ben and Aunt Lydia will be right there with you. Someone has to hold down the fort."

The evening progressed through dessert and then cleaning up the kitchen. They went from discussing John's chance of getting elected, to the prospects of Gram and Will getting married, to the baby Sara was expecting. It was an evening of family togetherness and conversations—and Rae could have listened all night.

When the evening came to an end, and she and Luke put on their jackets, Rae expressed her gratitude. "Thank you for a wonderful time, Sara."

"Thank you for coming. Sometimes I feel outnumbered by these guys." Sara motioned to the three men. "It's nice to have another woman around. Let's get together later in the week, okay?"

"I'd love that!"

"Better pull your collar up," Luke suggested as he opened the front door. "It's not getting any warmer outside!"

"Night!" Sara called as Rae and Luke hurried to his truck. It was cold, but thankfully the pickup's heater warmed up quickly.

"That was so nice. I've always wondered what it would be like to come from a large family like yours."

"It was fun." Luke adjusted the heater and grinned at her. "But being from a big family isn't always a joy. Sometimes it's a real pain."

"Really?"

"Really. But I wouldn't have it any other way."

"No, I don't think you would," Rae said softly. And neither would she, if they were her family. She felt so comfortable around them. While she'd caught Luke watching her a lot during the evening, he hadn't brought up the near kiss of the night before—and she certainly wasn't going to. Her thoughts kept returning to that moment in time when she understood, without a doubt, that she was in danger of caring way too much about this man.

❧

It's been a great night, Luke thought as he drove his aunt home. For the first time in a long time, he hadn't felt like a fifth wheel. Rae fit in with his family really well, and she seemed to like all of them. Well, except for Nora. Luke sighed. And possibly him.

As attracted as he was to her, he hadn't missed how she'd hugged the door of the pickup on the way to and from Jake's. And he couldn't blame her for keeping her distance. He wasn't sure exactly how she felt about him, especially after last night. He'd almost kissed her right there in his grandmother's kitchen. It was a wonder she'd even agreed to let him drive her to Jake's tonight. And he owed his aunt for that one.

"Aunt Nora, want me to come over and check out your car tomorrow?"

"If you have time. If not, I can call Ned's Auto Repair. He'll come out and tow it into town, if need be. I can drive the pickup. I just didn't much want to drive with the forecasters predicting snow if I could get a ride with you." She peered through the windshield. "I think they got it wrong, though."

"Oh, I don't know. That front may just be late in coming." He glanced over at his aunt. She seemed happy tonight. "How are things going with you and Michael?"

Her smile widened. "Very good. I'm so glad the Lord brought him into my life. You know, Luke, if we do get married and I move into town, my house will be empty. It's part of the family property. I think you should move into it."

"Me?" He loved Nora's home. Her sprawling ranch house

was much nicer and more modern than his. It had a huge kitchen, four bedrooms and three baths, a separate office, and an oversized pool out back.

"Yes, you," Nora insisted. "I should have moved into town and let you have it months ago. You're running the ranch property. My place is a little closer to town than yours, and you could let the foreman move into your house."

"Aunt Nora, I don't know what to say. I—"

"No need to say anything, Dear. Ben, Gram, and I have already talked about it. It's going to you."

Luke couldn't quite explain the bittersweet joy he was feeling. He'd never considered that he'd be inheriting Nora's place, although he loved it. It would be perfect to raise a family in. . .but it was awfully big for one person. Thoughts of Rae playing with Meggie came to mind. He shook his head slightly as if that would make the thought of Rae disappear. If only it were that easy.

ten

By the end of the week, Luke was pretty sure Rae was trying to avoid him. He'd looked for her at the diner on Tuesday evening but found she'd worked that morning. On Wednesday evening at church, Michael told him she was helping Dee out while she trained the new girl she'd just hired. When he stopped by the diner after church, Dee told him she'd sent Rae home minutes earlier.

Thursday morning, he was determined to track her down, but that was easier said than done. She wasn't at the diner; Dee said she was coming in later but didn't know where Rae might be until then.

Finally, Luke called Aunt Nora just to see if maybe they'd gone shopping, even though he doubted that was likely.

"No, Dear," Nora replied. "I've asked Rae to go shopping several times, but she's been so busy at the diner, and well. . .truthfully, Luke, I don't think Rae wants to spend her free time with me. I think sharing the occasional meal with Michael and me is about all she can handle of my company."

"I'm sorry, Aunt Nora." And he was. He wished Rae would give her a chance. She just didn't realize how much Nora had changed since Michael had come into her life.

"Don't be. I've handed it over to the Lord. But when you think of it, you can add your prayers to mine that she'll learn to like me one day."

"I'll do that."

"Thank you, Dear."

Frustrated at Rae's attitude toward his aunt and the fact that he couldn't find her, he decided to drop by his grandmother's on his way back to the ranch. And there, in the last place he'd thought to look, parked right out front, was Rae's car.

Luke pulled into the driveway and took a moment before he went inside. Releasing a deep breath, he sent up a prayer. *Father, please help me handle this right. I'm not sure why I feel the need to seek Rae out, but I do. If it's Your will that I do that, please help me to know why and what You would have me do about this attraction I feel for her. If she's not the stranger You've sent into my life, and if it's Your will that she go back home after the holidays, please just help me to get her out of my mind. And, Lord, please help her to accept Aunt Nora. In Jesus' name, amen.*

He didn't know what the Lord's plan for his life was, but he had to find out if Rae had a place in it—city girl or not. He hopped out of his truck, ran up the porch steps, and let himself in the front door. "Gram? You here?"

"Luke, we're in the kitchen; come on back."

Gram met him at the kitchen door and gave him a hug. "What are you doing here this time of day?"

"Can't I just come by and see how my favorite girl is doing?" He glanced over at the table where Rae was sitting with a pen and pad of paper and smiled. "Hi, Rae."

"Hi, Luke." The corners of her mouth turned up in a slight smile as she looked up at him.

"Dee's new waitress must be working out pretty good if you don't have to work."

Rae put the pen down and sat back in her chair. "She's working out real well. She's got a lot more experience than I do. I'm going to still help out if Dee needs me, but not as much. I'm feeling a little at loose ends now, though."

Luke didn't know what to say. He'd like to ask her to have lunch with him, but ever since the other night when he'd almost kissed her, he had no idea what to say to her. Now he settled for addressing both women. "So, what are you two ladies up to?"

"Rae is getting the butternut pound cake recipe I forgot to give her, and we're discussing the Thanksgiving menu. It's only a week away, you know." Gram motioned him over to the table. "Want some coffee?"

"Sure, but I can get it. You two get on with your planning. I'll be sure to add anything I think you leave out." He grabbed his favorite mug and filled it.

Gram chuckled. "I'm sure you will. Rest assured, pecan pie is at the top of the dessert list, along with pumpkin."

Luke took a seat at the round table in the bay window and grinned at Rae. "Well, then you've got the two most important items accounted for. You probably don't need my input after all."

"Rae is going to make my butternut cake, and Nora is making a chocolate cake. Lydia is making a couple of cream pies, and Sara is making her twenty-four-hour salad."

"I've never seen that many desserts at one meal." Rae shook her head. "And Gram has already given me the menu for the meal. How will anyone even have room for dessert? A gigantic turkey, a big ham, mashed potatoes, sweet potato casserole, green beans, dressing, gravy, rolls. . . And I know I'm missing a few more things."

"It's a big family, and we have several big eaters in it." Gram eyed Luke, who just grinned and shrugged.

"And everyone wants leftovers the next day," she continued. "Good thing we all live close. . . I'd never be able to cook it all here."

"I'll be more than happy to make something besides the cake. Just let me know what you need. I admit to being excited. I've never been to this big of a Thanksgiving dinner. After Mom passed away, Dad and I usually just made reservations at a nice restaurant and went there."

"Oh, this family would disown me if I suggested eating out! But it would be nice to dress up and—"

"Gram! Don't even think about it. We dress up a little—"

"Have someone to wait on me, for a change," Gram finished.

"I'll wait on you!" Luke exclaimed, knowing full well that the family dinner wasn't really at stake.

Gram shook her head, and both she and Rae laughed. "Calm down, Luke, we're eating here."

"Whew!" He grinned over at her. "I'm glad. We wouldn't have leftovers to take home."

"I can hardly remember having Thanksgiving leftovers."

"We'll make sure you have some to take home. After all that cooking, no one wants to spend a lot of time in the kitchen the next day."

"Is that the reason?" Luke asked. "I thought it was because leftovers taste even better than the original meal."

Luke saw the way Rae watched as he and his grandmother teased each other. Her smile seemed wistful to him. He felt a little sorry for her being an only child and not ever having had a big family Thanksgiving dinner. He couldn't even imagine what that would be like. He drained his cup and looked at the clock. It was time to get back to work. But he felt better. Rae hadn't left the country.

"Guess I'd better be going. You ladies have a good day. If I think of anything you've left out, I'll be sure to call."

"I'm sure you will," Gram came back with a grin. Luke gave her a kiss on the cheek and glanced over at Rae, but she seemed busy writing notes down. Was she remembering their near kiss of the other night?

"Bye, Rae. See you two later."

"Bye, Luke." She gave him a quick smile before giving her attention back to her list.

Luke strode out of the kitchen and to his pickup feeling relieved. Rae might be trying to avoid running into him, but it could only work so long. If nothing else, he'd be seeing her on Thanksgiving.

⁂

Rae's heartbeat slowly returned to normal. She certainly hadn't expected to see Luke at Gram's this morning. In fact, she'd been going out of her way to try *not* to run into him. Ever since Sunday night when she'd thought he was going to kiss her, and then the wonderful time she'd had with him the next night at Sara and Jake's, Rae hadn't been able to get him out of her mind—and she was striving very hard to do just that.

She already cared about Luke. But she couldn't afford to let the feelings grow. She just couldn't do that. Hurt as she'd been over the breakup with Paul, she had a feeling it would be far worse if she let herself care for Luke and things didn't work out. No. She had to keep her distance from him as best she could. It was the only way to protect her heart.

But keeping her distance was a challenge during the next week. Ben and Lydia had a party for John that Saturday evening, so that he could announce to family and friends that he was indeed running for United States senator. Lydia sat her between Luke and John, and it was a little hard to ignore him in such close proximity.

On Sunday evening there was Gram's Sunday night supper. Dad asked Luke to give Rae a ride while he drove Nora out to pick up the dessert she forgot to bring in with her. Thankfully it was a quick drive to Gram's from the church building, but there was a tension in the truck that couldn't be denied. Rae wondered if Luke was thinking about the last Sunday night supper as much as she was.

By Tuesday, when he and Jake met her and Sara for lunch at a fast-food place Meggie especially liked, Rae was beginning to wonder if the family was trying to get them together. But Sara's surprise at seeing Luke assured her that at least her new friend wasn't in on it, if that was the case. But Rae had a good time. Meggie kept them all entertained, and Luke and Jake spent most of the hour talking to the little girl..

On Wednesday, Rae helped out in the diner and was happy to find out that Dee had been invited to Gram's for Thanksgiving too.

"Oh, I'm so glad. I was wondering what you were going to do." Rae had found out early on that Dee had no family nearby. Maybe that was one reason Rae felt close to her.

"Ellie has been asking me for years. I always look forward to going. Some years it's been a little uncomfortable with John. . ."

Dee stopped midsentence, convincing Rae that there *was* something between her friend and Luke's cousin.

Dee bit her bottom lip and shook her head. Rae waited.

"I can't believe I let that slip." She chuckled and sat back in the booth and shrugged. "John and I used to date. And once in awhile we feel uncomfortable around each other. End of story."

Rae had an idea there was a lot more to the story, but obviously Dee didn't want to talk about it. And she didn't press. After all, she didn't want to go into her reasons for feeling uncomfortable around Luke. "Well, I'm glad you are going to be there. I've never been to a big family gathering, and I'm really excited about being part of it."

Dee grinned. "You are in for a treat. It's never dull when the Tanners and Brelands get together. Nor is it quiet."

❧

No, Rae thought the next afternoon. "Quiet" and "dull" were not words that could describe Thanksgiving at Gram's. "Noisy" and "fun" were. They ate around midafternoon, to give them time to make room for dessert later, John told her.

By the time they were gathered together for a prayer, the smells coming from the kitchen had several stomachs growling.

Gram asked Will to say the prayer, and they all bowed their heads.

"Our dear Father, who art in heaven, we thank You for our many blessings. And today we especially thank You that we are able to be together to enjoy this meal and the company of these loved ones—family and friends. Please bless those who prepared it, and thank You for providing it. And thank You, Father, for Your precious Son and our Savior, Jesus Christ. In His name we pray, amen."

"'Men," Meggie echoed, amid loving smiles and chuckles.

Everyone helped themselves to the bounty and found a place to sit. One table wouldn't hold them all, so a buffet was set up in the kitchen, and they ate wherever they could find a seat—not unlike a Sunday night supper. Rae found herself at the kitchen table with Luke, John, Dee, Jake, Sara, and Meggie in her high chair. Sitting between Dee and Sara, she was content just to listen to the family banter surrounding her.

She saw John whisper something to Dee; her friend blushed, making Rae wonder just what was up between them. They made a nice-looking couple. Luke's imperceptible nod in the couple's direction told her she wasn't the only one curious. But the wink Luke gave her when she glanced back at him had warmth stealing up her cheeks and her heart tumbling somewhere down around her stomach. She tried to avoid meeting his gaze by giving her full attention to the plate in front of her.

The meal was delicious, and Rae was thankful there would be time for it all to settle before they had dessert. The men spent the better part of the afternoon in front of the television set watching football, while the woman mostly congregated in the kitchen to clean up and talk about Christmas. Talk went from the menu for Christmas dinner, to how they planned on decorating their homes, to how the town decorated. There would be a nativity scene on the courthouse square across from the diner and lights in the trees. Each business downtown decorated, hoping to win first place in the annual contest.

"I've got to decide how I'm going to decorate the diner. I don't expect to win any kind of award, but I do want it to be pretty," Dee said. "Will you help me, Rae?"

"I'd be glad to. I love decorating for Christmas. Just let me know what you need me to do."

When the game went into halftime, Luke and Jake entered the kitchen demanding dessert. Rae could only laugh and shake her head when she saw them load up their dessert plates with several kinds of pie, cake, and Sara's famous salad.

She tried most everything herself, only in much smaller portions. By the time they'd finished having dessert and coffee, Rae was positive she wouldn't be able to eat for days. But sure enough, Gram sent leftovers home with everyone.

⁂

Dee had asked her to help out in the diner the next two days, and it didn't take long for Rae to understand why. Shoppers out to take advantage of the big holiday weekend sales kept them hopping. The diner was packed all day, but Rae enjoyed all the hustle and bustle, plus it almost kept her too busy to think about Luke. Almost. Thoughts of him managed to slip in no matter what she did.

By the time Sunday rolled around, Rae was ready for a nice, relaxing day, but she really didn't want to spend it with her dad and Nora. They seemed in a world of their own even when other people were around.

"Rae, if you don't have any plans for this afternoon, want to help me decorate the diner?" Dee asked as they headed toward the foyer.

Relieved that she had an excuse not to join her dad and Nora for lunch, Rae didn't have to think twice. "I'd love to. Just let me tell Dad I won't be joining him and Nora."

After promising them that she'd see them at evening services, she and Dee took off. They grabbed a hamburger from a fast-food place and then went to the new superstore to buy a tree with lights already on it, lighted garlands, ribbon, spare bulbs, and some ornaments. Dee had decided that she wanted to go with all-white lights after years of going with colored ones. She bought burgundy ribbons and decorations to match the color of the booths.

"Wow, that was easy," Dee said after setting the hinged tree up next to the jukebox. "I love real trees, but I feel safer having this one since I'll have it lit up for so long."

"I know what you mean. But this one looks very real." Rae helped spread the branches out. They added gold garland and the burgundy ornaments and stood back to inspect their work.

"It is pretty, isn't it?" Dee asked after plugging it in.

"It's beautiful." The glittering lights made everything sparkle even more.

They spent the rest of the afternoon putting the swag garlands in the windows, strategically arranging the power cords, and putting on the finishing touches. By the time they were through, they had to hurry to get to church in time for the evening service, and then it was on to Gram's for supper.

Rae rode over with Dee, but it was only after she spotted Luke talking to John outside that she hurried to the kitchen to help Gram. Thinking she'd safely avoided him, her breath caught in her throat when she spun around from setting a turkey casserole on the table to find him at her elbow.

"You are one hard lady to get in touch with. I tried to reach you this afternoon. John and I wanted to see if you and Dee would like to take in a movie with us."

"We were decorating the diner." But she wished she'd been at the movies with him.

"The one place I never thought to check. Michael told us you two were spending the afternoon together—just not where."

Rae sighed and shook her head. "I told him, but he seemed

to have his mind on Nora." As it always seemed to be lately. She wasn't even sure they'd noticed she was at church tonight.

"Rae, they—"

Gram interrupted him when she pronounced it was time to say a prayer and asked John to lead it.

Rae didn't think she wanted to hear what Luke had been about to say anyway. Everyone began helping themselves after the prayer, and she tried to avoid Luke, but it didn't work for long. He found her leaning against the sideboard in the dining room.

"Rae, we need to talk about Aunt Nora and your—"

Once again, Luke was interrupted; only this time it was by her dad. He smiled and clapped his hands together. "Everyone, please, could I have your attention?"

He gazed down at Nora and put his arm around her. "I have some wonderful news. This lovely lady has just agreed to be my wife, and we are thinking a Christmas wedding might be nice."

Rae's heart seemed to stop before it twisted in her chest and started up again with a deep, slow thud. Everyone was gathering around her dad and Nora, congratulating them, but she couldn't seem to move.

Luke touched her elbow as if to nudge her into action. "Rae—"

"No. I won't. . ." She pulled away from his touch and rushed into the kitchen, trying to sort her thoughts, catch her breath, and keep her tears at bay.

The door swung open, and Luke walked up behind her. "Rae. They love each other. Can't you be happy for them?"

Rae could only shake her head. She didn't trust herself to speak.

"Maybe it's time you grew up, Rae," Luke continued. "I know your dad is wonderful for my aunt. She's a different person since she met him. Can't you give them a chance to have a life together?"

"It *appears* that I don't have a choice. They've already made their decision." *Without even letting me know.*

"And you aren't going to make it easy on them, are you, Rae? You're acting like a child."

She whirled to face him. "You don't know what you're talking about, Luke. You didn't lose your mother in high school. You didn't have your betrothed dump you on the eve of your wedding for your best friend, and you didn't have your dad announce his engagement to the whole world without at least letting you know first!"

"Your dad loves you with all his heart, Rae. But he and Nora deserve to be happy." Luke reached out to her.

She held her hand out and backed up, brushing at the tears sliding down her cheek with her other. "No! I am not going to congratulate them. Don't you see? I can't!"

"It's all right, it's all right." Luke pulled her into his arms. "I didn't know you were hurting so badly, Rae. I didn't know."

Rae burrowed her face into his shoulder and sobbed.

"It's okay. Cry it out." Luke rubbed her shoulders and rocked her gently for several minutes before she pulled back slightly and looked up at him.

"I'm sorry. . .I. . . ," she whispered. Her heartbeat pounded in her ears at his nearness.

"It's going to be all right, Rae." He pulled her close again and tilted his head toward her. "It will be. . ." Luke's lips touched hers lightly at first. . .and lingered.

Rae kissed him back.

eleven

Rae's fingertips rested against Luke's chest, feeling the rapid beat of his heart. When he broke the kiss and released her, Rae suddenly felt bereft. How had she let herself respond to him like that? And why did he release her so abruptly? He'd been the one to initiate the kiss.

Even after the kitchen door swung open, it took a moment for her to get her bearings and realize that he must have known someone was about to come into the room.

Her dad and Nora entered the kitchen, and she had a sudden urge to turn and run. It was only Luke's steady gaze that helped her to regain her composure and stay put.

Dad came over and gathered her into his arms. "Rae, Honey, I'm so sorry I made the announcement about our engagement before I told you about it. I was just so happy Nora finally agreed to marry me that I wasn't thinking. But I should have told you first. Please forgive me."

Rae brushed at the tears on her cheeks and shook her head. "It's all right," she sniffled.

Nora reached out to touch her arm. "No, it's not. I am so very sorry, Rae. We just were not thinking right. The last thing I meant to do was start our relationship off by hurting you. We can put the wedding off for awhile."

Rae looked into the eyes of the woman who apparently would be her stepmother. Those same eyes that were shining with happiness only a few minutes ago now appeared to be clouded with concern. She seemed genuinely sorry that they hadn't told her first, and Rae began to regret being so unfair to Nora. The woman wasn't an ogre. She was simply a woman in love with a wonderful man.

She switched her attention to her dad and saw the pleading expression in his eyes. "Please, forgive us, Rae."

She suddenly realized that Luke had been right. It *was* time she grew up. Fresh tears threatened, and she willed them away. "No, I'm the one who should apologize. I'm sorry for acting like a child."

"Honey—"

"It's okay, Dad, but I. . ." Rae couldn't talk anymore. Wanting to get away from everyone, she backed toward the rear door, shaking her head.

"Rae, wait," Luke said.

"Honey, please." Her dad reached out and started after her.

"No, Michael. Let me," Nora implored. "Please. Just give me your car keys."

With tears blinding her, Rae ran out the back door into the chilly night air. She heard the screen door slam behind her as she hurried down the steps. Then she heard the door bang shut again.

"Rae! Wait," Nora called, sounding a little breathless. "Please."

Rae stopped in the middle of Gram's backyard. Nora sounded out of breath, and Rae had no idea where she was going anyway. She'd ridden over with Dee, and she didn't even have her purse with her.

Nora reached out and put her arm around Rae. "Come on. Let's go get some coffee. I know just the place."

Rae looked toward the kitchen and saw that her dad and Luke were watching from the porch. She couldn't face going back inside. She sniffled and nodded as Nora led her across the yard, then out to the street and her dad's car.

Nora handed her a box of tissues and adjusted the driver's seat to her height. She started the car and took off down the street. They didn't talk. Nora turned the radio on low and just drove around downtown for awhile.

"Okay now?" Nora asked after Rae stopped sniffing.

Rae blew her nose and nodded. "I'm sorry."

"So am I, Rae. Michael and I should have taken your feelings into consideration more." Nora drove back to the center of town and parked on the side street just outside the ice cream parlor. She switched the ignition off and turned to Rae. "They make a really wonderful vanilla cappuccino here. Want to try one?"

"That'll be fine." Rae got out on her side and joined Nora on the sidewalk. She was glad the shop wasn't very busy at the moment. She knew her face would be tear-streaked and her nose a bright red. She was ashamed of herself for being so unfair to her dad and Nora and for making such a scene in Gram's kitchen with Luke. And she was more than embarrassed at her response to his kiss. She felt herself flushing just thinking about it.

"Come on." Nora brought her out of reliving that kiss. "Let's get inside. It's getting cooler out."

Rae followed her into the shop, and Nora gave their order to the young woman she called Allie, who was working the counter. They waited while she fixed the cappuccinos right before their eyes. After Allie added a dollop of whipped cream, sprinkled cinnamon on the top of each mug, and handed them across the counter, they found a booth at the back of the room and sat down.

They spent the next few minutes sipping the rich, frothy drinks. Rae felt awkward and unsure of what to say to Nora, but she owed the woman the courtesy of listening to anything *she* might want to say.

"Rae, I really am so sorry we hurt you by making our announcement without talking to you first. I know that Michael feels horrible about it, and so do I. We should have—"

"Asked my permission?" Rae shook her head. "I don't think

so, Nora. You both have a right to be happy. I am sorry. I have been so closed-minded about how you feel about each other. I just. . . After Mom died and then the breakup with Paul. . .I guess I felt I was losing Dad to you. But Luke was right. I've been acting like a child." *And I've been blaming everyone, including the Lord, for my losses.* But deep down, she was certain that the Lord hadn't caused her mother's illness any more than He'd made Paul choose Laura over her. And she hadn't lost her dad. He might marry Nora and become her husband, but he would always be her daddy.

"Oh, Rae. Your dad is crazy about you. And I would never want to hurt his relationship with you. But I think I understand how you might be feeling. . .more than you know. Although you've handled the sorrows in your life much better than I handled mine."

Nora took a deep breath. "I'd been a widow a long time, but I had my son, Wade. And then Sara, after they married. I was about to become a grandmother. Then Wade was killed in the automobile accident, and Sara lost the baby and very nearly her life. But thank the good Lord, she came through. I felt like she was all I had left of my son."

Rae noticed the tears in Nora's eyes as she paused and took a sip from her cup. How could she have been so blind to the pain Nora had endured?

Nora put the cup back down and ran a finger around the rim, and Rae supposed she was trying to get her feelings under control before she continued. "When Jake moved back to town, and it became apparent that he and Sara were falling in love again, I thought I was losing everything. For awhile I even resented my own nephew because I thought he was trying to take her away from me. I'm ashamed to say so, but I tried to break them up." She shook her head. "I handled it horribly. My attitude very nearly cost me my relationship with Sara, with Jake, and the whole family."

"Sara never mentioned—"

Nora smiled and shook her head. "No, Sara wouldn't. She and Jake are very forgiving people. Actually, it was Jake who showed me how much he loved her by offering to let me be a grandmother to Meggie if I would just accept their marriage. And Sara let me know that if we were to have a relationship, I'd better accept his offer, because she was going to marry him and become Meggie's mommy. The Lord gave me one last chance to have a wonderful relationship with my family, and Michael helped me realize that I'd better take it. Without the Lord's love, forgiveness, and grace, I would be a lonely and bitter woman. Thankfully, He gave me a way to salvage what I almost threw away."

Nora stopped and smiled, tears gathering once more. "Now, Jake and Sara are expecting a baby, and I'll have another grandchild—not by blood but by love and family ties. Rae, please believe me. I would never try to take your mother's place in your heart. But I hope that one day you and I will have a good relationship."

By the time Nora finished, tears were streaming down Rae's cheeks again, and she grabbed several napkins from the dispenser on the table. "Nora, I am so sorry. I've been wallowing in my own self-pity as if I was the only one who ever suffered a loss. Please forgive me."

"Dear, there is nothing to forgive. I only told you all of this so that you would know you aren't the only one who ever felt that way—and that I do understand. My life has changed so very much this year, and to tell you the truth, I'm very nervous about this new change. I never thought I would marry again. I was afraid to love again. But the Lord brought Michael here, and I'm going to walk out in faith that He wants us to make a life together. It doesn't mean that we can't put the wedding off for awhile, though, if you'd be more comfortable with that."

Rae reached over and clasped one of Nora's manicured hands in her own. "No, Nora. There is no need to postpone the wedding. Since I'm here, I'd consider it an honor if you would allow me to help you with it."

She swallowed a lump in her throat as she watched Nora's reaction. Rae wiped at her eyes once more as Nora stifled a sob and smiled at the same time.

"Thank you. I would love that." Nora gave her hand a squeeze.

Rae squeezed back. She took a shaky breath before sipping her now lukewarm cappuccino.

※

They'd driven all over town trying to find Rae and Nora before Michael finally suggested checking out the ice cream parlor. They both breathed a sigh of relief when they spotted his car parked on the side street next to it.

After finding the two women in what appeared to be a serious conversation, they'd ordered coffee and waited unnoticed until Michael saw his daughter reach over to Nora, say a few words, and then smile.

Now, Luke watched as Michael approached the back booth where Rae and Nora were sitting, and he released a deep breath when Rae responded to her dad's hug. Her color seemed to heighten when Michael motioned for him to join them, and he felt a little flushed himself as he walked toward them. He couldn't get the kiss he and Rae had shared out of his mind. As he approached the table, he wondered if she was remembering it too.

He was relieved to see that both women smiled at each other when Michael asked, "I take it the wedding is on?"

"The wedding is on. Rae has graciously offered to help us plan it." Nora smiled up at her new fiancé.

"Thank you, Honey." Michael hugged Rae once more.

"I'm sorry, Daddy, I should have—"

"Shh. I'm just glad you are with us now."

Nora turned to Luke. "Can I get a ride home with you, Dear? I think Michael and Rae could use some time together."

"Of course, Aunt Nora. I'll be glad to take you home."

"No, Nora. This is a special night for you and Dad. You have plans to talk about, and I've put enough of a damper on things. Dad, go ahead and take Nora home."

"I'll see Rae home, Michael," Luke offered.

"Are you sure?" Nora asked Rae.

"I'm sure. You two go on, but could you loan me your key to the house, Dad? I don't have my purse with me."

Nora handed Michael his key chain, and he removed the house key while she slipped out of the booth and stopped to embrace Rae. Michael handed his daughter the key and gave her a kiss before he and Nora headed out the door.

Feeling a little uncomfortable and not knowing quite what to say, Luke took the seat Nora had vacated and stole a glance at Rae, who was gazing down into her cup. "That was nice of you, Rae. I'm glad you and Aunt Nora came to an understanding."

"You were right." Rae finally raised her gaze to meet his.

"About what?"

"That I needed to grow up." She bit her bottom lip, bringing the kiss back to Luke's mind.

He shook his head and sighed. "Rae, I'm sorry. I shouldn't have said that. I didn't know where you were coming from, how hurt you'd been—"

"No. You were right. They deserve to be happy. And I've been acting like a spoiled brat. I'm sorry I made such a scene. . . ."

Relieved that she hadn't apologized for the kiss, Luke reached across the table and pulled one of her hands between both of his. "Rae, you could have made things much harder on them. You didn't. You just didn't. . .try to. . ."

"Accept that they love each other? No. I tried to fight it instead." Rae slipped her hand out of his clasp and leaned back against the booth.

Luke sensed she was distancing herself from him more than just physically. "Well, you have had some heartache of your own. The timing must have seemed really bad to you. I'm sorry you've been hurt, Rae."

"So have lots of other people. My selfish behavior would have deeply disappointed my mother. She'd want me to be happy for Dad, just as she would be. I know that might sound strange, but do you see what I mean?"

"I do. And I have a feeling she'd be real proud of you now. I certainly am."

"Thank you, Luke." She closed her eyes and began rubbing her temple. "I have a colossal headache. Would you mind taking me home now?"

Much as Luke wanted to talk about what had happened between the two of them in Gram's kitchen, now wasn't the time. Rae appeared emotionally exhausted, and she didn't seem to want to meet his gaze. "Of course not. Come on."

He stood and waited for her to slide out of the booth. Once outside, he helped her into his truck and turned the heater on. The silence between them was anything but comfortable, and Luke wondered if it was because they were both thinking of the kiss they'd shared. He sure couldn't get it out of his mind. When he stopped in the drive at Michael's front door, he wanted nothing more than to pull her into his arms and tell her everything would be all right—but he didn't have the chance.

"Don't worry about seeing me to the door," Rae said, quickly opening the door. "It's cold out, and I'm just going to dash in. Thanks for the ride, Luke."

Before Luke could even say good night, she'd run to the front door, unlocked it, and hurried inside. Obviously, she didn't want to discuss what had happened between them tonight.

Luke drove toward home telling himself to be patient. Rae wasn't going anywhere just yet. She'd committed to helping Nora with the wedding. Right now he'd just be glad she seemed to be accepting Michael and Aunt Nora's engagement.

There would be time to talk about how their relationship had changed. And it had changed tonight. Of that he had no doubt.

೭ఇ

Luke drove off, and Rae let out a huge sigh of relief as she leaned against the front door, thankful he hadn't brought up the kiss. She was mortified enough as it was and still couldn't believe she'd acted so childishly. But she'd responded *and kissed him back*. Rae shook her head. She'd been trying to block out thoughts of the kiss all evening. . .to no avail. Even during the emotional roller coaster of an evening talking to Nora, thoughts of that kiss had been hovering at the back of her mind.

From the moment he'd pulled her into his arms and his lips touched hers, she'd felt a joy she couldn't explain even now. It felt as if that was where she'd always belonged, and everything in her shouted that she was on the verge of falling in love with Luke—and that he might, just might, feel the same way about her.

Yet now, she was sure it was only wishful thinking on her part. Her feelings were deceiving her. More than likely, after her tirade, Luke had kissed her only because he felt sorry for her. And pity was the last thing she wanted from Luke Breland.

She should probably just pack up and go back to Albuquerque, but she couldn't do that now. She'd promised to help plan the wedding and she meant to keep her promise.

Rae pushed away from the door, rubbing her throbbing temple. Her headache wasn't getting any better with all these thoughts going round and round in her head. She went to the kitchen to find some aspirin before heading to her room.

After a shower, Rae got ready for bed. She was tired. It'd been a long, hard day, and she'd had to face some unpleasant truths about herself. But before she could go to sleep, there was one more thing she had to do. She got down on her knees beside the bed and prayed.

Dear Father, please forgive me for blaming You for all the heartache I've felt. I was wrong. You are the One who has held me up and kept me going through it all. I'm the one who made everything harder than it needed to be. Oh, I told myself that I was trusting You to lead me, but I wasn't.

Please forgive me. . .for not talking to You like I used to. . .for not looking to You for guidance as I should have. And for hurting Dad and Nora. I should have been happy they found each other. I realize now that bearing the heartache of losing someone doesn't mean we'll never love or be happy again. Nora will make Dad a good wife; I know she will. She loves him very much. Please help me to make it up to them.

And, Father, I promise to try to do Your will, to let You lead me from now on. Please help me to lean on You the way I was taught to do. And please, Father, help me not to fall in love with Luke. I'm not ready to risk being hurt again. It's just too soon. Thank You for my many blessings, Father. In Jesus' name, amen.

Rae crawled into bed feeling as if a weight had been lifted off her shoulders. Oh, she still had feelings for Luke that needed to be dealt with, but she felt closer to the Lord than she had in months, and she was certain He would help her. She closed her eyes and drifted off to sleep.

twelve

Dad greeted her with a big smile when she walked into the kitchen the next morning. "Hi, Honey! You aren't working this morning, are you?"

"No." Rae shook her head. "Dee's new waitress is working out very well. I may see if she needs any more help decorating, though."

She took a mug out of the cabinet and filled it with coffee before joining him at the kitchen island where he was eating a bowl of cereal. "I want to plan a surprise bridal shower for Nora, and I thought I'd better get an early start."

Her dad hugged her. "Thank you, Rae. That will mean so much to Nora."

"Just don't tell her. I want it to be a surprise."

"All right, I promise not to tell." He took a drink of coffee. "I know she'll love it, but I don't think there's anything she'll need to set up housekeeping, Honey."

"That's not the point, Dad. I want to welcome her into our family, like we've been welcomed into hers."

"Rae, you don't know how much that means to me."

"I'm sorry it took me so long to come around. But I see how happy you are with Nora, Dad. How can I not want that for you?" Rae wished she'd come to that realization sooner rather than later.

"Your mom would be as proud of you today as I am, Rae," he said huskily.

"Thanks, Dad." She cleared the knot forming in her throat and continued. "Anyway, I'm going to stop at the diner and see Dee. After that I'm heading over to Gram's. Have you and Nora set a date yet?"

"We're thinking after Christmas. Maybe even New Year's Eve."

"Now that would be a way to start the New Year, wouldn't it? But that really doesn't give us much time to plan."

"I know. But I think Nora just wants a simple wedding. And. . .I just want to marry Nora."

"I'll be sure to call her a little later in the morning." Rae rummaged through the built-in desk in the kitchen for a pad of paper. Finding what she wanted, she stuffed everything into her purse. "The sooner we get started, the quicker this will all come together."

"Thank you, Honey."

"You're welcome. I do want you to be happy, Dad."

"And I want the same for you."

"I know."

"I know there is someone out there for you, Honey."

Only one person came to mind, and Rae tried to put him right back out of it. She sure hoped she didn't run into Luke today. She was still embarrassed about the night before. "Let's just get you married first, Dad."

"That's a deal."

Rae chuckled and kissed him on the cheek before heading out to her car. She left the house feeling better than she had in months. Now if she could just stay busy enough to keep thoughts of kissing Luke out of her mind, she *might* get through the holidays.

She was surprised to find that the thought of going home to Albuquerque held no appeal anymore. There was no doubt in her mind that she was over the breakup with Paul and that she could continue to work at Zia High School. She really liked Sweet Springs and the people here. But this town held another problem for he—in the form of one Luke Breland.

Dear Lord, please help me to put that kiss into perspective. Luke was feeling sorry for me and probably just trying to comfort me. I'm sure that's all it was. But I don't want his pity. And I wasn't comforting him. I responded, and I don't know how to act the next time I see him. Please help me to keep my distance from him for the next few days so that maybe I can get past this. . . growing feeling I have for him. Please help me, Lord. In Jesus' name, amen.

Rae's plan to stop at the diner changed quickly when she spotted Luke's pickup parked outside. She just couldn't face him right now. Her heart was already thudding against her ribs at just the prospect of running into him. She had to avoid that as long as she could, but it wasn't going to be possible forever. Not with her dad marrying his aunt. She was going to have to deal with it all sooner or later. Right now, she preferred later.

She passed by the front door and hoped Luke didn't decide to come out right at that moment. She turned left at the corner and headed for Gram's. Surely he wouldn't show up there this morning.

Gram welcomed her with open arms and led her back to the kitchen. "How are you this morning, Dear?"

Rae was sure she was concerned about her reaction to her dad and Nora's announcement the night before, and she was glad she could reassure the older woman. "I'm fine, Gram. The Lord helped me put things into perspective, and Nora helped me see how much she loves Dad. I'm truly sorry my initial response wasn't appropriate."

"Oh, I don't think that many people noticed. I'm so glad you've accepted their engagement. They are very good for each other. Nora is a different person since she met Michael." Gram chuckled. "And we're all eternally grateful that the Lord brought him into her life."

Rae smiled. Even though she was positive Gram knew everything Nora had told her the night before, she didn't want to repeat any of Nora's confidences. "I think Dad is just as grateful. What I wanted to talk to you about—and I need to talk to Sara and Lydia too—is that I'd like to give Nora a surprise wedding shower."

"Oh, she'd love that, Rae!" Gram walked over to the wall phone. "Pour yourself some coffee, and I'll give them both a call. We can have this planned by lunchtime!"

&.

Luke took his time over his breakfast, hoping to run into Rae. At some point they were going to have to talk about that kiss. But after he'd been there for over an hour, he finally asked about her.

"I don't know where she is." Dee refilled his coffee cup. "I thought she would be in to help me put the finishing touches on the decorations this morning, but I haven't heard from her. What do you think of them so far?"

"They're great. What else could you possibly need to do?"

Dee grinned at him. "Actually, not much else. I do have something *you* can help me with, though."

"Oh, what's that?"

Dee went behind the counter and came back with thumb-tacks and two sprigs of mistletoe. "I won't have to drag out a ladder if you'll put these up for me."

Luke grinned. He'd sure like to meet Rae under one of these sprigs. "Sure. Where do you want them?"

"How about one over the door and. . ." She looked around the diner and shrugged. "Where do else you think?"

Luke glanced around. "How about over the jukebox or above the cash register?"

Dee grinned at him and shook her head. "The cash register might be a tad too obvious, don't you think, Luke?"

He laughed. "You read me too well, Dee."

"I've seen the way you look at Rae. I'm just not sure she has."

"Me either." Luke sighed and took the mistletoe and tacks from Dee. "We'll go with over the jukebox."

Dee watched as he reached up and stuck the first clump in

the ceiling over the jukebox and then one over the door. "That'll work. Thanks, Luke."

"You're welcome."

"What are you welcome for?" John asked as he came through the doorway.

Luke sat back down at his table and grinned at Dee. "I just did a favor for Dee, that's all."

"Oh, what was that?" John joined him at his table.

Luke pointed to the ceiling above the door his cousin had just come through.

"Oh, that should make for some interesting people watching," John said and chuckled.

"Sure should." Dee brought him his usual cup of coffee.

"Hi, Dee. The place looks real nice and Christmassy."

"Thanks. Rae helped me."

John blew on the hot liquid in his cup. "I just saw her pass by. I thought she might be coming here, but I guess not."

So much for his hope of running into Rae. Once again, he suspected she was avoiding him. Well, she couldn't steer clear of him forever. They were bound to run into each sooner or later. But, as far as he was concerned, sooner would certainly be better.

❧

Gram was right. By lunchtime they had Nora's shower planned. It would be held at Michael's house. Sara and Lydia had brought Meggie over, and Rae was officially welcomed into the family.

"I can't tell you how happy we are about Nora and Michael," Lydia said. "We've all been praying this would happen."

"And I'm glad you are happy about it too, Rae. . .and that you are going to be part of the family now," Sara added.

"Thank you. You've all made me feel so welcomed."

"When one marries into this family—be it Breland or

Tanner—they and their family automatically become part of our family."

"I have another reason to love Nora, then—besides the fact that she loves Dad and he loves her. I've always wanted to be part of a large family."

Lydia laughed. "Your dream has come true, Rae. 'Cause this one is that. There are many you haven't even met yet. It may be larger than you wished for."

Rae shook her head. "No. I don't think that's possible."

Now they cleared the table of all shower plans and set it for lunch while Gram tossed a large salad together. Rae had called Nora earlier and issued the invitation from Gram that they all meet for lunch to start planning the wedding, just in case she came by early and saw all the cars in the drive and wondered what was going on.

But there really wasn't much chance of that, Sara told her. Nora loved keeping to a schedule, and she rarely was late for anything. Nor did she like others being late. It appeared Sara was right when, at twelve o'clock sharp, they heard the front door open.

"I'm here! I picked up the most wonderful crusty rolls to go with the salad—" Nora had barely cleared the door before she was enveloped in congratulatory hugs.

"I am so happy for you, Nora," Lydia said. "You know we've been hoping this would happen!"

"So have I!" Nora exclaimed and laughed. She hugged Rae and smiled. "I'm so glad I'm going to have you all to help me plan this wedding!"

"Well, let's have lunch and then we'll get started," Gram suggested.

After they'd all taken a seat, they joined hands and Sara said the blessing, thanking the Lord for their many blessings, and especially for bringing Michael into Nora's life. Nora asked what they thought about New Year's Eve for the wedding. They all agreed that it would be perfect.

"We want to have it before Rae goes home. It would be hard to go back and forth every week for dress fittings and everything," Nora said.

"Dress fittings?"

"Why, yes. I'd like Lydia to be my matron of honor, if she'll accept."

"You know I will." Lydia grinned from across the table.

"And I'd like you and Sara to be bridesmaids, if you would, Rae."

"I'd be honored." Rae smiled at her stepmother-to-be. After the way she'd acted, she really didn't deserve the honor Nora was bestowing on her.

"So would I. Oh, this is going to be so much fun!"

"Ellie, I hope you'll serve as mother of the bride, since my mother is no longer with us."

"You don't even have to ask, Nora."

"Thank you. Anyway, we don't want anything elaborate, hopefully making it easier to do while Rae is here."

"Rae, you know you really ought to think about moving here permanently," Sara said. "There's a job opening for a history teacher at the high school."

"Really?"

"Uh-huh. The present teacher's husband has been trans-ferred, and they need someone fairly soon."

"Oh, Rae!" Nora exclaimed. "Do you know how happy that would make your dad? What a wonderful wedding present it would be!"

"You think so?"

"Of course it would!" Lydia agreed.

"And what better way to get to know your big, new family than to live in the same town?"

Rae chuckled and shook her head. "I don't know, Gram. I always thought I was a city girl. Never thought I'd live in a little town like Sweet Springs."

"Oh, you'd love it here. You have a built-in family, a wonderful church family, and Meggie can always use another aunt. Wouldn't hurt to check it out," Sara said, forking a piece of lettuce off of her plate.

"I. . ." What could she say? If it weren't for the fact that Luke lived here, she'd apply in a minute. And what was worse? To move back to Albuquerque, to an empty house and friends that hadn't even called to see how she was? At least here she would have people who cared. And if it got hard to be around Luke, the Lord would help her with that. Here she would have the family she'd always dreamed of having. "I'll think about it. Maybe I will apply."

"Wouldn't hurt," Gram added. "You could stay with me and try it for the next semester, until you made up your mind—"

"Ellie, she can stay with us," said Nora. "I know Michael would be pleased."

Rae shook her head. "No, I don't think so. I know Dad loves me, Nora, and you are sweet to suggest it, but the last thing newlyweds need is an adult child living with them!"

"Gram's idea is a good one, though," Sara said. "And I think the school board would be elated to have someone with your experience take the job. They called me only because they know me; I don't have any high school teaching experience."

The more Rae thought about it, the more the idea appealed to her. There was only one problem as far as she could see, and his name was Luke Breland. She hadn't been able to get him out of her mind since she'd entered the kitchen; how could she possibly ignore thoughts of him if they were living in the same town?

❧

On Tuesday evening Luke found out that Rae had been one or two steps ahead of him the day before when he stopped by and begged a meal from Sara and Jake, hoping to find out if Rae had left town.

Sara was full of news about the plans they'd made to give Aunt Nora a surprise shower. "It was Rae's idea. I'm so glad she's taking Nora and Michael's engagement well."

That comment only served to remind Luke of the night they'd announced it and the kiss he and Rae had shared in Gram's kitchen. As if he needed reminding. It was about all he'd thought of the past few days. And evidently, from the way she seemed to be trying to avoid running into him, he'd blown his chances with her because of it. At least she hadn't left town.

"Why so glum, little brother?" Jake asked when even Meggie's stunts couldn't make him laugh. The best she could get from her uncle Luke was a smile.

"Guess it's just the gloomy winter weather."

"Luke, it's been sunny all day," Sara said as she cleared the table and brought a freshly baked apple pie to the table.

"Oh. Well, maybe it's just the time of year. You know how some people get depressed around Christmastime."

"You *love* Christmas," Jake said. "You love everything about it—especially buying us all things you know we'll have to stand in line to take back."

"Maybe I'm coming down with something," Luke said. He could have bitten his tongue when Jake leaned back in his chair and studied him for a few minutes. His brother could read him well.

"Maybe you're *lovesick*."

Sara whirled around from the cabinet where she'd been getting dessert plates and forks. "Luke?"

She came back to the table and sat down across from him. "Who?"

"Sara. You know who." Jake began to chuckle.

She clasped her hand briefly over her mouth. "Rae? Oh, Luke, that's wonderful!"

"I did not say I was lovesick. That came from your husband."

Sara cut into the pie and served them each a piece. "So you aren't attracted to Rae?"

Luke let out a deep breath and shook his head. Family. He'd said enough already. He wasn't saying any more. He took a bite of pie and watched Jake grin and wink at his wife.

He passed Nora's on the way home, wondering if he'd ever move in. He felt lonely enough in his small ranch house. He wasn't sure he could handle rambling around in one more than twice the size of his.

Wednesday morning, he went into town and found he'd missed Rae at the diner by only minutes. Dee told him that she and Nora and Sara had taken off for Roswell on the hunt for dresses for the wedding.

Frustrated that he hadn't seen Rae since Sunday night, Luke went home and spent the afternoon on horseback. It was a beautiful, sunny day, and he always found solace and peace on the wide-open range. But he didn't find it today. He didn't know what to do about his feelings for Rae, and so he rode leisurely, seeking guidance from the Lord.

Father, I don't know what to do. I'm attracted to Rae, city girl that she is. And I don't know if I should pursue her or leave her alone. It appears that's what she wants me to do, yet I can't forget the way she responded to my kiss. Please, Father, let me know if she's the one You've brought me, or if I need to keep my distance. If she is my "stranger," please help me to know. It's in Jesus' name I ask this, amen.

Luke rode for most of the afternoon before heading back to his ranch. He brushed down his horse, feeling more at peace than he had in days—although he still didn't know what to do about Rae. He'd know. . .in the Lord's time.

He took a shower and made it to the diner for supper. Rae wasn't there, but then he didn't expect her to be. That was how his week was going. She probably wouldn't even be at church tonight.

At church, it seemed everyone was talking about Nora and Michael's announcement. He was happy for them. He couldn't help wondering who in his family would marry next. It seemed even Will and Gram would be exchanging vows before he got around to it.

John walked up behind him. "All this wedding talk. Do you ever feel like we're the last two bachelors in town?"

Luke laughed. "We certainly are in *this* family, aren't we?"

But as he walked into the sanctuary, it suddenly became crystal clear to him that he wanted his bachelor status to change—and with whom he wanted to make that change. Rae was sitting beside Aunt Nora. Just the sight of her had his stomach doing a somersault and his heartbeat hammering in his ears. Oh, yeah, Jake was right. He was about as lovesick as a cowboy could get.

thirteen

Luke took a seat a few pews behind Rae and tried to concentrate on the Bible class that was just beginning. His life sure had been simpler before Rae came into town, but it hadn't been near as exciting. He felt more alive than he had in a long, long time. And it all was due to the blue-eyed, dark-haired woman sitting right in the middle of his family. She seemed happier than he'd ever seen her, and he was grateful that she and Nora had come to an understanding.

After the closing prayer, Luke tried to get to Rae, but with all the people coming up to congratulate Michael and Nora on their engagement, she'd gone in the other direction. He thought about taking a shortcut through the pews to get to her, but she seemed a woman on a mission as he watched her stop to talk to one lady after another. It probably had something to do with that wedding shower Sara said she was planning.

Not one to give up, he backtracked to the fellowship hall. She'd have to come through there to leave. He mingled and talked to first one person and then another, keeping his eye on Rae's progress through the window that looked into the sanctuary.

"Want to go get a cup of coffee at the diner?" John asked.

"Sure," Luke said. "Just give me a minute, and I'll see if Rae wants to go too." But when he peered through the window once more, he couldn't find her. He'd only taken his gaze off her for a minute, and she couldn't have left without him seeing her. Letting out a frustrated breath, he headed back into the sanctuary through the other door and almost plowed right into the woman Rae was whispering to.

He reached out to steady Harriet Johnson to keep her from falling. "Oh, I'm so sorry, Mrs. Johnson. I wasn't watching where I was going."

"It's all right, Luke. You almost tripped me once before, when you were a child. We all know how clumsy you used to be. Guess you haven't completely outgrown it." With that she straightened the handbag she had slung over her shoulder, winked at Rae, and lumbered through the doors.

Luke glanced down at Rae and saw the sparkle in her eyes. He could tell she was trying to hold back a giggle. He chuckled. "Go ahead and laugh. She's right. That's what happens when people know you from the time you were born. They don't forget a thing. Nor do they let you."

Rae released the giggle and shook her head. "If you could just have seen the expression on your face. . ."

Luke didn't care how silly he might have looked. He was just glad she was talking to him. "John and I are going to the diner for coffee. Want to come?"

The smile disappeared. "Oh, thanks, but I'm taking Gram home so we can finish up some plans."

"Okay," Luke said. "How about going to a movie with John and me tomorrow night?"

"I'm sorry, Luke." Rae shook her head. "We're giving Nora a surprise shower this week. It's short notice but with the wedding to plan and Christmas coming. . . Maybe Dad would like to go, though. The shower is at his house, and he probably needs a place to hang out."

Luke didn't think she was sorry. He thought she was relieved. But here and now wasn't the time to get into it. "We'll ask him and see if he wants to go."

"Thanks. Guess I'd better get going." Rae waved and hurried over to Gram.

Luke sighed, forced himself to smile, and waved at his grandmother. He felt a tap on his shoulder and turned to find John.

"Rae has other plans?"

"Yeah, she's busy with Gram tonight. Let's go." He'd spend the evening watching John and Dee try to ignore how they felt about each other. John was right. Like it or not, it seemed they were to remain the last two bachelors in the family.

❧

Rae didn't know whether she was relieved or disappointed that she couldn't go to the movies with Luke, but it was probably for the best, anyway. She wasn't sure she could hide the fact that he set her pulse racing each time she saw him. And she was afraid that if she spent too much time around him—although that was exactly what she wanted to do—he'd be able to tell that she was falling in love with him. That is, if her response to his kiss hadn't already done that.

Right now, she was just glad she had plenty to do. Staying busy with shower, wedding, and Christmas plans wouldn't keep thoughts of Luke out of her mind, but it would give her an excuse to get some distance when she felt she was close to exposing how she felt about him.

But now, as she and Sara put out the cake and floral arrangement on the dining room table in preparation for Nora's surprise shower, she found herself wondering where he was and what he was doing.

"What are all the men doing tonight? Dad said he was going over to your house after he gets Nora here, but Luke mentioned asking him to go to a movie."

"Luke is out of town. He and Uncle Ben made a spur-of-the-moment trip to a livestock sale in Las Cruces. But John was going to join Dad and Michael over at my house and hang out with Jake. I baked a cake and made sure they had plenty of microwave popcorn and snacks on hand. They'll have a good time."

"I'm sure they will," Rae said, bringing dishes of nuts and mints to the table. She was a little disconcerted to find out

Luke had left town and she didn't know it. Then she chided herself—she'd been going in the other direction every time she saw him lately. Why should he tell her something like that?

The doorbell rang, and she opened the door for the arrival of Gram, Lydia, and Dee. They'd parked down the street, as everyone had agreed to do, and walked up to Dad's house. Before long, all the guests had arrived and were staking out a spot to hide for when Dad brought Nora to the door.

Rae turned out all the lights, except for the one in the kitchen they left on all the time. They tried to say quiet, giggling softly at Gram's occasional reminders to be quieter.

Rae heard her dad fumble his key in the lock, as they'd planned for him to do, and everyone waited for the door to open. He stood aside so that Nora could enter.

"Surprise!" everyone shouted in unison as she walked into the entryway.

"Oh!" Nora laughed and whirled around to husband-to-be. "You were in on this, weren't you?"

"Of course I was. Rae knows I can keep a secret." He looked around at all the smiling women and grinned. "But I'm going to let her take over now. Have fun, everyone."

Nora kissed him before he slipped out the door. She was drawn into the great room where she was placed in the seat of honor. She grinned at Rae and Sara. "I can't believe you had time to put this together as busy as I've been keeping you!"

"They are younger than we are, Nora," Lydia said laughingly.

The next few hours passed quickly while Nora opened beautifully wrapped packages and colorful bags. There were monogramed bath towels and linens, picture frames, scented candles, and crystal candleholders.

Lydia and Gram gave her a beautiful handmade afghan; Sara gave her two mugs, one with *Nana* engraved on it for her and the other with *Papa* for Rae's father.

"Oh, how adorable!"

"I hope Michael realizes that when he marries you, he automatically becomes Meggie and the new baby's adopted grandpa," Sara said.

Nora chuckled. "Oh, yes, he does."

Dee gave her gift certificates for free meals at the diner, amid much laughter. Most of them were fully aware that cooking wasn't Nora's favorite thing.

But the present Rae waited anxiously for Nora to open was the one from her. She hoped it would show that she truly had come to care about her future stepmother.

Nora unwrapped the present, smiling up at Rae as she did. Nora gasped when she opened the box to find a beautiful leather Bible, with *Nora Wellington* engraved on the front in gold letters.

Inside, Rae had written, *To Nora, who has made my dad a very happy man. My prayer is for God to bless your marriage and for you to have many happy years together. I'm honored to have you as my stepmother. Love, Rae*

"Oh, Rae." Nora held the Bible to her heart and looked up at Rae with tears in her eyes. "Thank you. I can't tell you how happy. . ."

Rae fought her own tears and bent down to embrace her. "You're welcome. I mean every word."

There were a few more presents to open, and then the women enjoyed the refreshments. By the end of the evening, Rae didn't just feel as though she was part of a new, big family; she felt she was part of the community.

The rest of the week sped by as she helped Nora pick out invitations, flowers, and a cake. The wedding would be at church, but the reception was going to be held at Gram's. It's what Gram wanted, and Sara, Lydia, and Rae all promised to help.

There seemed to be so much going on, and so many festivities planned for the month, Rae hardly knew what day it was. But she did know she missed seeing Luke. His absence hadn't done a thing to dispel the memory of their kiss. Rae's pulse still raced each time she thought about it. And she thought about it often.

On Saturday night, Rae talked her dad and Nora into a quiet evening at home to put up his Christmas tree. With the wedding at the end of the month, Nora had decided against putting up one at her house, but she obviously enjoyed helping decorate the house she'd be living in by the New Year.

They ordered pizza and spent several hours just getting the tree up and decorated, singing along with Christmas carols on a CD. The tree was enormous and almost reached the ceiling, and once all the lights were on it, the garland added, and the ornaments put on, it lit up the whole room.

When her dad took Nora home, Rae curled up in the big armchair facing the tree to gaze at the lights that glittered and shined, bouncing off the ornaments and garland. She made herself some hot chocolate and listened to Christmas music, wondering what it would be like to share the evening with Luke. She'd been trying not to think of him, but it was a losing battle. She'd thought of little else the past few days.

It was there that her dad found her when he got home. "You always have loved sitting in a darkened room with only the Christmas lights on. It's good to know you haven't outgrown it."

She smiled at him as he sat down in his chair. "I don't think I ever will. I do love the lights. It would be like Christmas every day if we all let our light shine in the world the way we are meant to, wouldn't it?"

Dad nodded. "It would. I know you've made the lights shine brighter for my and Nora's Christmas, Rae."

"Took me long enough to come around, didn't it?"

"It doesn't matter how long it took; it happened. Now, tell me. What do you want for Christmas, Honey?"

"Just to see you and Nora happy, Dad."

"Well, you'll get that. But what else?"

What else? How about a life here in Sweet Springs, with a long, tall cowboy named Luke? She couldn't tell her dad that—she couldn't tell anyone that. But she had to be honest with herself. She was in love with Luke Breland, and a life with him was what she wanted.

Rae didn't hold out much hope that he could return her feelings. He'd seen her selfishness up close in his grandmother's kitchen, and all she'd done before that was complain and put down the land and the town he loved. How could he possibly care about her? How was she going to hide her feelings from him?

&

Luke and Uncle Ben didn't get back into town until late Saturday night. It'd been a good trip as far as business was concerned. But it'd been a complete failure as far as getting Rae Wellington out of his mind, and that was the primary reason he'd suggested it.

He barely made it to church on time the next day, and when he saw Rae laughing and talking to Aunt Nora right before the worship service started, he was struck by how much she seemed to have changed since his first meeting with her. She'd gone from resenting his aunt to looking forward to being her stepdaughter. She seemed completely at home here, and happy, as she talked with one of the elders of the churchand Richard Shelby, the superintendent of schools.

When he watched Meggie crawl from Sara's to Nora's lap, then across to Rae, Luke couldn't deny it any longer—the city girl had his heart in her hands, and he just prayed she wouldn't crush it.

Sometime in the coming week, he was going to have to find her and talk to her. It was time they cleared the air. He had to find out where they stood. Rae had responded to his kiss. He hadn't imagined it. And he couldn't forget it.

But finding a way to be alone with her so that they could talk remained frustrating at best. That afternoon, another shower for Nora was being given by some of the civic groups she volunteered for. Naturally, Rae was invited too.

At Gram's supper that night, Rae seemed to be avoiding the kitchen by staying in the dining room and talking to everyone except him. Tired of fighting what seemed to be a losing battle to get her alone and fatigued from his trip, Luke left early. Maybe Rae wasn't meant for him, and if that was the case, he just prayed the Lord would let him know soon so he could get off of the emotional seesaw he seemed to be stuck on.

After making himself concentrate on business until nearly noon the next day, Luke headed into town on the pretense of meeting John for lunch. He knew the real reason he'd accepted the invitation was with the hope of running into Rae somewhere along the way. But, he'd promised himself that he would leave all of that in the Lord's hands. Only He knew where she'd be today.

Luke opened the door to go in and collided with a small woman on her way out.

"Oh, I'm sorry; are you all right?" he asked, reaching out to steady her. He gazed down at the woman whose shoulders he held, and his heart collided with his chest bone. After hunting for Rae all over town for days, here she was. At last.

"I'm fine." She sounded a little breathless. "How about you?"

"I'm good." *Now that I've found you, better than good.* Luke just stood there staring at her, blocking the door until he heard Dee clear her throat. He glanced at his friend and realized she was looking at the mistletoe above Rae's head. He grinned and tightened his hold on Rae's arm. Ducking his head quickly before she had a chance to pull away, he planted a quick kiss on her soft lips, but not so quick that she didn't have time to respond. His heart seemed to soar when she did.

Luke heard several handclaps and chuckles in the background. He raised his head.

"I. . .ah. . .what?" Rae seemed a little confused.

"Merry Christmas," Luke whispered, surprised at the huskiness in his voice.

"Look above your head," one of Dee's regulars yelled out amid more laughter.

"Oh." Rae glanced up, and color flooded her cheeks as she glanced back at him. "Merry Christmas."

Her lips turned up in a smile that didn't quite reach her eyes, and Luke had a feeling he'd messed up. Again. She'd responded; he was certain she had. Did she think he'd only kissed her because they were under the mistletoe? "Rae, we need to talk. Do you have time for a cup of coffee?"

She shook her head. "I don't have time right now."

"Where are you going in such a hurry?" he asked, guiding Rae out of the way so that one of Dee's customers could enter the diner.

"I'm on my way to pick up Nora's invitations. With the wedding right after Christmas, we really need to get them addressed and mailed out as soon as possible." She seemed to be looking anywhere but at him as she continued. "The printer called her this morning, and Nora asked me to pick them up. She and Lydia are going to Roswell to try on more dresses. Sara and I found ours, but they're still shopping."

"Do you need a ride?" Maybe they could talk if he could just get her to himself.

Rae shook her head. "No, thanks. My car is down by the printer's, and I'd better be getting down there. Sara is meeting me at Gram's so we can get started addressing them. See you later."

"Later." Luke sighed as she hurried out the door. He sat

down at a table Dee was just cleaning off and shook his head.

"Sorry, Luke. I thought I was helping your cause," Dee said.

He shook his head and sighed. "I don't think anything is going to help my cause. I can't get her to stand still long enough to even talk to me about anything except that wedding. Certainly not about how I feel about her."

"And how do you feel?"

Luke ran his hand over his face. Had he really given himself away like that? He shrugged. "It doesn't matter. She's not interested in finding out."

"I wouldn't be quite so quick to jump to that conclusion, Luke. She's just very busy helping with the wedding plans. She wants to show Nora and Michael that she's happy for them. Once the wedding is over with, she won't be so busy."

"And she'll go back to Albuquerque."

"Luke. . ." Dee seemed about to say something else, but she shook her head before continuing. "Even if she goes back to Albuquerque, she'll be coming to visit her dad. It's not like you won't see her anymore. And Albuquerque isn't *that* far away. I didn't think you were one to give up so easily, Cowboy."

Luke felt a glimmer of hope start to grow within him. Dee was right. Rae would be back. It *wasn't* as if he'd never see again. And it wasn't as if he hadn't felt her lips linger on his—if only for a moment—when he kissed her under the mistletoe.

There was no doubt in his mind how he felt about her. And until she told him to get lost, there *was* hope. He inclined his head and grinned at Dee. "You are right. I don't give up easily. I certainly shouldn't give up until I find out where I stand."

"Now that's the Luke I know and love," Dee said as John walked up behind her.

"Am I interrupting something here?" John asked, his left

eyebrow arching almost into his hairline.

Luke chuckled at his cousin's reaction to Dee's statement but sought to put his mind at ease. "Dee's giving advice to the lovelorn."

"Ahh," John said, his eyebrow easing back to its normal position. "And you are the lovelorn one, I presume?"

Luke glanced at Dee, then back to John. Jake and Sara were aware of how he felt—now Dee. Luke grinned at his cousin. Why not tell him too? Maybe it was time to enlist the help of his family and friends. It sure couldn't hurt.

"Oh, why deny it? It seems everyone knows how I feel about Rae—except her."

"Well, when are you going to let her know?" John sat down across from him.

"He's having a hard time getting her alone long enough," Dee explained.

"Oh. Well, you know, if I remember right, the family had to help Jake along in his romance with Sara. You know we'd all be glad to help you out too."

"Well, I'm not family," Dee said, "but I'll certainly do my part."

fourteen

Rae fought tears all the way to the printer's. When she'd gone into the diner to tell Dee what she'd done, she'd been very excited. After being approached by the superintendent of schools at church the day before—and much prayer—she'd applied for the teaching job Sara told her about. She had a feeling she just might get it. Teasing that it might just be her wedding present for her dad, as Sara had suggested, she'd asked Dee not to say anything about it just in case she didn't get the job.

Then she'd run into Luke. . .and he'd kissed her right there in Dee's diner. When her lips met his, she knew she'd made the right decision. But the elation Rae felt at Luke's kiss quickly deflated when she realized that he'd kissed her because of the mistletoe.

Now, as she picked up the invitations and headed back to her car, she told herself she had to face the truth. She really wanted the job and to live in this town. Most of all, she wanted Luke to care about her. She was pretty sure she could have the first two. But the third, and the one she wanted with all her heart, was totally out of her control. She had to give it over to the Lord. Only He knew the outcome, and He was in control.

Dear Lord, please help me here. I love Luke, but I don't know how he feels about me. I would love for us to have a life together, but after the way I've treated his aunt, he probably thinks I'm the most spoiled, selfish woman he knows. He told me that I need to grow up, and he was right. Mostly, I need to grow as Your child, Lord. Please help me to do that and to accept Your will in my life, no matter what it is. In Jesus' name, amen.

By the time Rae got to Gram's with the invitations, she was at peace for the moment and anxious to share her news about the job. They were waiting for her in the kitchen.

Rae set the box of invitations on the table and went to pour herself a cup of coffee from Gram's always-full pot, marveling at how comfortable she felt in this house and with these women. If she and Luke weren't meant to be, it wasn't going to matter if she lived in Albuquerque or here. Running back to the city wouldn't get them out of each other's lives. She might have to live with heartache again, but at least here she'd have a family and a church family to draw strength from. And most importantly, God would help her handle it all. Yes, He would.

She twisted away from the cabinet and grinned at the two women at the table.

Sara was watching her closely. "What's up, Rae? You look like you are about to burst."

Rae grinned. "I am. I've waited all morning to get over here and tell you two my news."

"And what news is that, Dear?" Gram asked, setting a plate of cookies on the table.

"I found a wedding present for Dad."

"Oh? What did you get him?" Sara took a seat at the table and began to unpack the invitations.

"Well, I haven't signed the contract yet, but I'm hoping that I will very soon."

"Okay, Rae, I'm curious now! What have you found?"

"Just what you suggested, Sara. A move here—if I get that teaching job I applied for."

Gram chuckled and hugged her. "I'm so glad, Rae. It will be wonderful to have you around all the time!"

"You did it! Oh, how wonderful!" Sara laughed happily and jumped up to give her a squeeze as soon as Gram let her go. "Michael and Nora are going to be thrilled!"

"I certainly hope so. Just don't say anything to them okay?

I may not get the job, but I want to surprise them, if I do."

"Mum's the word," Gram said. "Remember, you are welcome to stay with me until you find a place of your own."

"Thank you, Gram. That is so generous of you!"

"I'll be glad to have you here. It's a big house for one person."

"Why don't you and Dad just get married, Gram?" Sara asked. "Then neither of you would have to be alone."

She chuckled. "Well, you never know. We might just do that one of these days."

Sara laughed and shook her head. "I'll believe it when I see it."

They spent the next several hours addressing Nora's invitations and talking about the reception menu, the wedding, and anything else that came to mind. It was wonderful to sit around the table and talk, feeling that she was part of this family.

When she answered her cell phone, she expected it to be Nora checking to see if she'd picked up the invitations. Rae glanced at the phone's screen and gave Sara and Gram a nervous grin.

"Hello, this is Rae."

"Hello, Rae. This is Richard Shelby. I've just had a meeting with the board. We would like to offer you a contract if you are still interested in teaching history for us."

It was time to make a decision. "Oh, yes, Mr. Shelby, I do want the job."

"Could you be ready to start by January fifteenth?"

"Yes, I can."

She watched Sara and Gram hug each other while she concluded the conversation, thanking the superintendent and agreeing to come in later in the week to sign the contract. She'd barely ended the call when they all shared a three-way embrace.

"Now, remember, don't tell anyone. I'll tell Dad and Nora at Christmas—or right before their wedding. I'm just not sure exactly when."

"We won't tell anyone," Sara assured her, sitting back down at the table. "But this is such wonderful news—it won't be easy keeping it quiet!"

"I know. I'll probably be the one to give it away!" Rae laughed as she joined Sara and Gram at the table.

"When will you go back to pick up your things?" Gram asked.

"I don't start teaching until the fifteenth. . .so I'll probably go back right after the wedding." She grinned at the two women sitting across from her. "I do love teaching. . . I can't wait to get back to it!"

❧

Standing right outside the kitchen door, Luke overheard Rae say she'd probably go back right after the wedding, and his heart seemed to dive right down to the pit of his stomach. He'd been hoping she was beginning to like Sweet Springs better and that she would decide to stay. Evidently she was still determined to go back to home. He tried to hide his disappointment as he pushed the door open and stepped into the kitchen.

"Hi, ladies! Need any help?"

Sara jumped when she saw Luke standing in the doorway.

"Luke! You scared us," Gram said, chuckling and putting her hand to her chest.

"I called out, but I guess you didn't hear me." Admittedly, he hadn't called out very loud. He was half afraid Rae would run out the back door before he could get to the kitchen, even though she'd told him where she'd be. But what did it matter now? She planned on going back to Albuquerque anyway.

No. He wasn't going to think negatively. She might well leave after Christmas, but she'd be back. There was hope. And he had family to help his cause. He just might have to wait for a more opportune time to let her know how he felt and find out if she might feel the same way. For now, with all this wedding stuff going on, he figured if he ever hoped to get to talk to her, he might as well jump in and help out.

"Come on in, Luke. We won't turn down free help," Sara said.

"What do you need me to do?" He poured himself a cup of coffee and took a seat at the table.

"Here you go." Gram pushed a pile of addressed envelopes with their invitations toward him. "Just put these in the envelopes and seal them."

"Sounds easy enough." Luke took an invitation and slid it into the envelope. But when he licked the flap, the face he made had everyone laughing. He shuddered. "Eeew! Yuck! I see why you gave me this job! Gram, do you have something else I can moisten these with?"

"Oh, I'm sorry, Luke. Wait just a minute." She put a small sponge in a saucer with a little water, then set it on the table in front of Luke. "Try this."

"After I get this awful taste out of my mouth," Luke said, going to the sink for a drink of water. He drained the glass and turned around to find Rae watching him, a half smile on her face. His heart jumped in his chest. Was she thinking about the kiss they'd shared that morning? Or the one they'd shared here? His grandmother's kitchen was fast becoming his favorite room in her house. Luke smiled and couldn't resist winking at her.

Rae quickly ducked her head, but not before he saw the delicate color creeping up her neck. His heart pounded and he prayed silently. *Dear Lord, please let me be reading Rae right. I know she responds to my kisses. I think she cares, or at least could care about me. Help me to know for sure.*

Luke had to tear his gaze away from Rae, and when he did, it was to see Sara and Gram glancing from Rae to him, trying to hide their amusement. He'd been around these two long enough to know they read him very well. He hoped they didn't comment on what it was they'd decided he was thinking. He let out a sigh of relief when neither said anything and rejoined them at the table where he stuffed, sealed, and stamped envelopes for the next half hour.

He tried to act surprised when Dee called to see if Rae could come help her out at the diner for a few hours. "I thought her new waitress was working out."

"She had to leave early today, and Jen is going to be late for some reason," Rae said, stacking the envelopes she'd addressed with the others. "There aren't too many left to do, and Nora and Lydia should be here any minute to help finish up."

She grabbed her purse and hugged both Sara and Gram. "I'll talk you later. Bye, Luke."

He watched her leave before giving his attention to his grandmother and Sara.

"Okay, what's up, Luke?" Sara asked. "We know you didn't come here just to help out."

"Well. . .I have something to ask you, but if Aunt Nora and Aunt Lydia are due here, I'll wait until I have you all in one place."

"Now you really have our curiosity piqued." Gram got up to refill their coffee cups. "Wouldn't have anything to do with Rae, would it?"

"It might."

But before he had a chance to say more, Nora and Lydia arrived; they also seemed surprised to find him there in the middle of the afternoon.

"Why, Luke, I know you are happy for me, but I really didn't expect you to pitch in and help like this," Nora said, giving him a hug.

"Before you get too mushy about it, wait. I think we'd better find out what his motive is," Sara said.

"Oh?" Lydia asked.

Luke gave them all what he hoped was his most persuasive smile. "I need to ask you all a favor."

Nora and Lydia took a seat at the table. The four women gave him their undivided attention. It was time to find out if the ladies in his life were going to help him win over the woman he loved.

❧

With Christmas fast approaching and the wedding the week after, Rae couldn't remember ever being busier. It was only a few days until Christmas, and she was running errands for Nora, helping her dad move things around to make room for the items Nora planned to move in—not to mention trying to get some Christmas shopping done.

Rae had signed the contract with the school board and let Zia High School know she wouldn't be coming back. She couldn't wait until the family gathering at Gram's to tell her dad and Nora. It was too hard to keep it quiet, and she didn't want to wait until the wedding. Besides, she was having second thoughts, and she needed her dad's encouragement.

She wondered what Luke would say when he found out she was going to move here. Would it even matter to him? She prayed that she wouldn't have to spend the rest of her life doing what she'd been doing for the past few weeks—trying to avoid being around him so he didn't guess how she felt about him.

Having admitted to herself that she was in love with him, she felt anyone who saw them together would know, and until she thought she could hide the effect he had on her—the shaky hands, the telltale blushing—she'd avoid him. So far, with all the errands and shopping she had to do, it hadn't been too hard.

She'd helped Dee out several afternoons so she could get some shopping done. And she'd thoroughly enjoyed the Christmas festivities in the small town. The downtown area had its Christmas decorations judging, and Rae was almost as thrilled as Dee when the diner won first place. The church held its annual Christmas caroling party for young families and children, and she helped with the younger children, including Meggie. The toddler had taken quite a liking to Rae, and the feeling was mutual.

Sara asked her over for dinner one evening, but Rae had to ask for a rain check because she and her dad were going to Roswell to do some Christmas shopping.

On the weekend before Christmas, the diner was swamped with shoppers, and Dee asked her to help out for a few hours. She'd only been there for a half hour when a customer knocked a glass off his table, and in picking it up, Rae accidentally cut herself. Charlie was going off duty, so he rushed her to the emergency room.

A few stitches and a half hour later, she was on her way home with her dad. Groggy from the pain medicine they'd given her, she thought about Nora's family gathering for the next night at Gram's and was glad she'd spent the last few nights baking the cookies and making the candy she'd promised to take. She just hoped she'd have the bandage off before the wedding—or at the very least that the bouquet she'd be carrying would hide it.

❧

Luke was more frustrated than ever. His family had agreed to help him find an opportunity to talk to Rae alone, but nothing was working out quite the way they'd planned.

Tonight seemed be the final straw. Dee was trying to do her part by asking Rae to help her out in the diner so that Luke could catch her there. But before he arrived, Rae had cut herself on a broken glass. Dee told him Charlie had taken her to the emergency room, and she'd called Michael to let him know. But by the time Luke got to the hospital, Rae had been released and sent home with Michael. When he'd called to see how she was, Michael told him she was sleeping.

Giving up for the night and driving home, he let out a frustrated sigh. It seemed he was just going to have to cool his heels and wait on the Lord to provide him an opportunity to talk to Rae.

By the next night, when the family gathered at Gram's for

supper and to decorate the fresh-cut tree she always insisted on, Luke had convinced himself that either Rae wouldn't feel like coming or she'd have some last-minute thing to do.

But when she and Michael showed up, he prayed that somehow—with all his family here—surely he would find out if there was a chance she could ever return his feelings.

While Will and Jake set the tree up, the rest of the family went through boxes of favorite decorations. It seemed everyone had a special one they remembered from years past. Once the lights were in place, everyone helped hang the ornaments. Then Gram handed each one a box of old-fashioned tinsel to put on the finishing touch.

That always took longer than anything else, because Gram insisted they do it one strand at a time. But they'd only been draping the long, silver strands on the tree for a few minutes before Nora said, "Oh, no!"

"What is it? What's wrong?" Michael asked.

"I just remembered the ornaments I made for you and Rae to put on Ellie's tree. How could I have forgotten to bring them?"

"Well, it's not like you haven't had anything on your mind, Dear," Gram said. "With all the wedding planning and everything—"

"Don't worry about it, Nora. We can put them on later," Michael assured her.

"No, they need to be put on tonight. Luke, would you be a dear and go get them for me?"

"Now?" Luke was trying to maneuver himself over to stand beside Rae. The last thing he wanted to do was go out to his aunt's ranch. This was the closest he'd been to Rae in days. He frowned at Nora with a refusal on the tip of his tongue— and saw her slight nod in Rae's direction.

"Rae, would you ride with him, please? I wrapped them in that paper you helped me pick out the other day. You'll know which ones they are."

Thank you, Aunt Nora! Luke held his breath waiting for Rae to answer.

"Oh, well. . ." Rae bit her bottom lip and glanced at Luke.

"Come on. It won't take long. By the time we get back, maybe they'll have all the tinsel on."

"Okay, I'll go." Rae chuckled. "I'm not real good with tinsel. I usually end up throwing it on. Just let me get my jacket."

Luke helped her slip it on over her bandaged hand, and they hurried to his truck. He helped her get in and latch her seat belt, then hurried around to jump in and switch on the heater. Now that he had her alone, he didn't know quite what to say. They'd gone several miles in silence before either of them spoke.

"How is your hand feeling? I called last night after I heard about your accident, but Michael told me you were sleeping."

Rae rubbed her bandaged hand. "Dad told me you called. Thanks for being concerned. It doesn't hurt too much today. It was a clean cut."

"That's good. Will you have the stitches out for the wedding?"

"I certainly hope so."

Luke pulled into his aunt's driveway, aggravated at himself for not asking what he really wanted to know: Could Rae ever care for him? They hurried up to the door, and Luke unlocked it with his key. For as long as he could remember, each member of the family had keys to each other's homes. Now as he held the door open for Rae to enter, he wondered again if he could move into this house and live in it by himself.

Rae walked into the kitchen and turned to him. "This is such a nice home. I love it. Will Nora sell it now that she's marrying Dad?"

Seeing her here in the kitchen that would soon be his, Luke realized he didn't want to live in this house unless it was with Rae. He shrugged. "It's part of the family property. She and Uncle Ben have told me it's mine now. But I don't know. It's awfully big for one person."

"Nora lives here and she's just one person, but it does sort of call out for a family, doesn't it? Maybe one day you. . ." Rae cut her sentence short, leaving Luke wondering what she'd been about to say.

She walked over to the kitchen table that held a small pile of presents Nora had wrapped, and she picked out two small ones. "Got them. Guess we'd better be getting back. They are probably waiting supper for us."

She headed out the back door, and Luke wondered what made him think he'd find out how she felt about him once they *were* alone. Now that he finally had her to himself, he didn't know how to even begin. Maybe it was because he wasn't sure he would like her answer. They were halfway back to his grandmother's before he finally asked the one question that was most important to him at the moment. "I. . .guess you'll be going back to Albuquerque after the wedding?"

"Ah. . .yes. Most probably the day after."

Luke's heart twisted in his chest. It was what he expected to hear but had hoped, with all his heart, not to. He was more than disappointed. He'd wanted her to say she wasn't going, that she was staying here. But still, as Dee had pointed out, Rae would be back. He had to hold on to that.

"Will you be coming back during summer breaks?" He glanced over at Rae, but she was gazing out the side window.

"Oh, I'll be back."

Luke smiled. He could live with that answer. For now.

They arrived back at his grandmother's to find the tree finished and the staircase banister decorated. While he watched Rae hang her ornament on Gram's tree, Sara whispered in his ear. He looked up to see several clumps of mistletoe that'd been added to the décor, but after the last time he'd kissed Rae under one of those, even though she'd responded, he wasn't sure he should try it again.

After everyone helped themselves to the light supper of soup and sandwiches that'd been set out in the dining room, they all gathered back in the living room to sing Christmas carols and exchange the presents they'd drawn names for this same time last year. Most of the time they were joke presents, and Luke loved it. But tonight his heart was heavy at the thought of Rae leaving soon, and he barely paid attention to what was going on, until she handed a present to her dad and Nora.

"This is for you both. I couldn't wait any longer to give it to you. I hope you like it." She seemed a little nervous as her dad and Nora began to open the gift. It seemed to be a bundle of papers tied up into a scroll of sorts.

When Michael glanced up from reading the papers he'd unwrapped, it was obvious he was thrilled with whatever Rae had gotten them. Nora seemed exceptionally pleased too.

"Honey, is this for real?" Michael asked.

Rae smiled and nodded. "It is. I hope you won't get tired of me."

"No way!" Michael grabbed her in a bear hug. He waved the papers in his hand. "She's going to move here. This is a signed contract to teach history at Sweet Springs High School!"

Luke's heart soared. Rae was staying. He watched her being hugged by half his family—and found her gaze on him, as if she were trying to gauge his reaction. Well, she wasn't going to have to wait long to find out just how he felt—only until he could talk to her alone so as not to have the whole family watching. Once the attention moved to Sara, who was opening a present from Jake, Luke strode purposefully over to Rae. "That's wonderful news about you moving here, Rae."

She looked at him and smiled. This time it reached her eyes. "Thank you. I'm happy about it."

"Why didn't you tell me on the way here?"

She shrugged. "I didn't know what you would think. I—"

"I'd like to tell you. Come on." Luke took her left hand in his and pulled her across the room and into the deserted kitchen. Turning her into his arms, he touched his forehead to hers. "Rae, I think it's time we talked."

"About what?" She pulled back and gazed up into his eyes, and Luke had to let her know how he felt. If she couldn't return his feelings, he'd count on the Lord to help him through it, but he had to know where they stood. Now.

"About how we feel about one another. . . How I feel about you." She didn't pull away and he continued. "I know now that you *are* the stranger I prayed the Lord would send me— on the very day we met. And I know that I love you, Rae."

Luke heard her small intake of breath and saw tears gather in her eyes. He didn't know what kind of tears they were, but he had to finish. "I know you are a city girl, but I think you've learned to love my town. . .could you. . .do you think you could ever learn to love me, Rae?"

"Oh, Luke," she breathed. "I've been in love with you almost from the moment we met. I—"

He didn't wait for her to finish. He'd heard all he needed to hear. He dipped his head, and his lips claimed hers in a kiss meant to assure her that he loved her—with all his heart. She responded in just the way he'd dreamed she would. He didn't care who came in the kitchen this time. Rae loved him. *Thank You, Lord!*

When the kiss ended, Luke whispered in her ear, "Will you marry me, Rae? If the commute into school gets too hard from Nora's. . ." He embraced her and corrected himself, "From *our* ranch, we'll move into town—"

"Shh," Rae whispered, touching his lips with her finger-tips. "As long as I'm coming home to you, Luke, the commute will be just fine. And yes, I'll marry you." She stood on tiptoe and kissed him.

Luke inclined his head and pulled her close. His lips met hers, and he sent up a prayer of thanksgiving to the Lord for bringing his "stranger" to town.

epilogue

It was the kind of Christmas Rae thought only happened in movies. But it was real. Luke bought her rings on Christmas Eve and put the engagement ring on her finger Christmas Day. Once they told the family they were getting married, nothing would do for Dad and Nora than for Rae and Luke to share their wedding day.

"After all," Nora told them, "the arrangements are all made. All you'll need to do, Rae, is find a dress and make arrangements for a bouquet. You and Luke can call any friends you might want to invite—if they haven't already been invited to our wedding. Think of the nice surprise in store for them!"

After discussing it for about five minutes, Rae and Luke happily agreed. She didn't have to start teaching until the middle of January. That would give them time for a honeymoon.

It'd been the most wonderful, hectic week in her life; she made lists, phone calls, and shopped. Sara and Lydia had run all kinds of errands for her. She'd exchanged her bridesmaid's dress for the wedding dress she'd fallen in love with at the shop where Nora had found hers. It was simple and elegant, with a dropped bodice made up of white lace and seed pearls, and a flowing white satin skirt. Another wedding cake had to be ordered, but Gram insisted on making both of the grooms' cakes.

The week passed in a blur of activity, and now as she and Luke stood beside her dad and Nora, looking out at the guests who'd witnessed their double wedding, it was hard to believe she was a married woman.

Gram sat there with Will, wiping tears from her eyes. Rae had promised Sara that she and Luke would join the family in encouraging those two lovely people to be the next to marry. Ben and Lydia had served as best man and matron of honor for her dad and Nora, while Sara and Jake had stood up as her and Luke's attendants. Dee sat with John, and they watched over Meggie. Head over heels in love, Rae couldn't help hoping that one day Dee and John might walk down this aisle themselves.

She smiled as David introduced Dad and Nora to the guests. Then it was her and Luke's turn. Rae gazed up into the eyes of her new husband, and her heart felt as if it might explode with joy when David introduced them as Mr. and Mrs. Lucas Breland.

Luke pulled her arm through the crook in his elbow and clasped her left hand tightly as they followed the older couple back down the aisle. Once in the fellowship hall, she and Luke hugged her dad and his aunt before turning back to each other.

Luke pulled her into his embrace and whispered in her ear, "I love you, Rae."

"And I love you. . .with all my heart."

Rae's arms encircled her husband's neck as he leaned forward to kiss her. Just before her lips met his, she thanked the Lord above for the family ties that brought her and this handsome cowboy into each other's lives.

A Letter To Our Readers

Dear Reader:

In order that we might better contribute to your reading enjoyment, we would appreciate your taking a few minutes to respond to the following questions. We welcome your comments and read each form and letter we receive. When completed, please return to the following:

Fiction Editor
Heartsong Presents
PO Box 719
Uhrichsville, Ohio 44683

1. Did you enjoy reading *Family Ties* by Janet Lee Barton?
   ❑ Very much! I would like to see more books by this author!
   ❑ Moderately. I would have enjoyed it more if

   _____

   _____

   _____

2. Are you a member of **Heartsong Presents**? ❑ Yes ❑ No
   If no, where did you purchase this book? _____

   _____

3. How would you rate, on a scale from 1 (poor) to 5 (superior),
   the cover design? _____

4. On a scale from 1 (poor) to 10 (superior), please rate the
   following elements.

   ____ Heroine   ____ Plot
   ____ Hero   ____ Inspirational theme
   ____ Setting   ____ Secondary characters

5. These characters were special because?_____
_____
_____

6. How has this book inspired your life?_____
_____
_____

7. What settings would you like to see covered in future
   Heartsong Presents books? _____
   _____
   _____

8. What are some inspirational themes you would like to see
   treated in future books? _____
   _____
   _____

9. Would you be interested in reading other **Heartsong
   Presents** titles? ❑ Yes   ❑ No

10. Please check your age range:
    ❑ Under 18   ❑ 18-24
    ❑ 25-34   ❑ 35-45
    ❑ 46-55   ❑ Over 55

Name_____
Occupation _____
Address _____
City_____ State_____ Zip_____

----- Heartsong -----

Presents

*H*EARTSONG ❤ PRESENTS

Love Stories
Are Rated G!

That's for godly, gratifying, and of course, great! If you love a thrilling love story but don't appreciate the sordidness of some popular paperback romances, **Heartsong Presents** is for you. In fact, **Heartsong Presents** is the premiere inspirational romance book club featuring love stories where Christian faith is the primary ingredient in a marriage relationship.

Sign up today to receive your first set of four, never-before-published Christian romances. Send no money now; you will receive a bill with the first shipment. You may cancel at any time without obligation, and if you aren't completely satisfied with any selection, you may return the books for an immediate refund!

Imagine. . .four new romances every four weeks—two historical, two contemporary—with men and women like you who long to meet the one God has chosen as the love of their lives. . .all for the low price of $10.99 postpaid.

To join, simply complete the coupon below and mail to the address provided. **Heartsong Presents** romances are rated G for another reason: They'll arrive Godspeed!

YES! Sign me up for Hearts❤ng!

NEW MEMBERSHIPS WILL BE SHIPPED IMMEDIATELY!
Send no money now. We'll bill you only $10.99 post-paid with your first shipment of four books. Or for faster action, call toll free 1-800-847-8270.

NAME _____

ADDRESS _____

CITY_____ STATE_____ ZIP_____

MAIL TO: HEARTSONG PRESENTS, P.O. Box 721, Uhrichsville, Ohio 44683
or visit www.heartsongpresents.com